A TASTE OF CHRISTMAS

"What an attractive room," Christopher said. "It has a homelike look to it. Oh, and here is our mince pie. I see it's almost midnight, so if we manage matters properly, we can consume our good luck ration for today *and* to-morrow in one fell swoop."

Ellie made a light reply to this. Together she and Christopher laughed and joked as they ate their mince pie, but all the while she was very much aware they were alone—as alone as they had been under the sky a few minutes before, now that the maid had gone. And the bunch of mistletoe was still hanging there, right in plain view.

"Superb," Christopher declared. "The very best mince pie I have eaten in my life."

"I'm so glad you liked it," said Ellie. "I shall be sure to relay the compliment to Mama." Suddenly nervous, she sprang to her feet. "I suppose we had better be getting back to the Winwoods'."

"Miss Roswell, you will be thinking me a terribly forward fellow," he said, "but there's a bunch of mistletoe hanging over the hearth there, and I am strongly tempted to take advantage of it. Would you think me an unmitigated bounder if I stole a kiss—just one kiss for luck?"

"No," said Ellie in a soft voice. "I would not think you a bounder at all."

Putting an arm   r led
her beneath the   d his
lips to hers . . . .

Fr   *Reed*

BOOK YOUR PLACE ON OUR WEBSITE AND MAKE THE READING CONNECTION!

We've created a customized website just for our very special readers, where you can get the inside scoop on everything that's going on with Zebra, Pinnacle and Kensington books.

When you come online, you'll have the exciting opportunity to:

- View covers of upcoming books
- Read sample chapters
- Learn about our future publishing schedule (listed by publication month *and author*)
- Find out when your favorite authors will be visiting a city near you
- Search for and order backlist books from our online catalog
- Check out author bios and background information
- Send e-mail to your favorite authors
- Meet the Kensington staff online
- Join us in weekly chats with authors, readers and other guests
- Get writing guidelines
- AND MUCH MORE!

**Visit our website at
http://www.kensingtonbooks.com**

A TASTE OF CHRISTMAS

Alice Holden
Debbie Raleigh
Joy Reed

ZEBRA BOOKS
KENSINGTON PUBLISHING CORP.
http://www.kensingtonbooks.com

CONTENTS

LORD NABOB'S CONVERSION

Alice Holden

Chapter 1

"You there, Rushmore!"

The shrill female voice arrested Justin Sinclair, the Earl of Rushmore, at the door to the card room where he had a scheduled rendezvous with Henry Chasen, his boyhood friend. Frowning, he sought out his rude summoner in the ballroom where the musicians were arranging their sheet music on the metal stands for the next set of dances. He swore under his breath. *Lady Willmer*. He was surprised she was still alive, for she must be ninety if she was a day.

For a moment Justin thought to ignore his ancient nemesis, but too many patrons of the Carnbury Village assembly had their eyes riveted on him in frank curiosity and their ears cocked to hear his every utterance.

Swallowing his irritation, he strolled to where the baroness, whom he had not seen in twelve years, sat leaning forward on a hard wooden chair. Her gnarled hands cupped the gold knob of a mahogany cane.

The earl kept his deep voice neutral as he said, "Lady Willmer," and looked down at her from his above average height. His blue eyes were cool in a handsome face bronzed by the hot suns of India.

"You recognize me, then," she cackled, obviously delighted. "When you ran off like a whipped puppy from Sinclair Hall, you were a mumbling fribble of eighteen years of age who had nothing to say for yourself."

Justin remembered. He had been a frequent victim of Lady Willmer's acid tongue as a feckless youth, but the uncertainties and fears he had suffered when his father had put a bullet in his brain to avoid debtor's prison had vanished years ago. No longer did he have to walk on eggs around her.

He managed a false smile and said, "I am older and wiser and not so easily wounded these days." He almost added *by bullies like you.*

But her wrinkled lips crimped as though she had read his mind, and her small black eyes narrowed. Justin did not give her time to retort. He had said as much as he cared to to her. Even politeness did not oblige him to engage in a prolonged conversation.

He quickly claimed he was late for his appointment with Henry Chasen and took one step from her side, but stopped short when he chanced to glance down at the young woman who sat in the chair next to her. The honey-blonde vision was gazing up at him with her mouth quirked into a semblance of a smile.

Justin drew in a breath. Their eyes locked for a duration that lasted far beyond the bounds of propriety. He immediately realized two things about her: She was very attractive, and she radiated confidence, despite being attired in a faded pale pink gown that had to be a hundred years old.

Justin watched a question mark develop in her soft brown eyes, the color of warm brandy. Her well-defined brows thrust up ever so slowly, as if she were asking, *Well, what do you think of me?*

When he grinned his approval with a devil-may-care smile, a charming chuckle bubbled from her naturally pink lips.

Justin unconsciously put aside his meeting with Henry and made to speak to her, but Lady Willmer clicked her tongue repressively and banged her cane on the floor.

"Dinah," she commanded, "I'm thirsty. Fetch me a glass of the grape punch."

Justin could not take his eyes from the young woman as she rose and walked away from him to do Lady Willmer's bidding. She was truly lovely, with a fine, trim little figure and a graceful carriage.

Lady Willmer sniffed loudly. "You apparently have acquired the bottom to restore respectability to the Sinclair name, Rushmore," she said with a sneer, "but amusing yourself with a female of no consequence, a nobody who is quite beneath your aristocratic touch, will not enhance your luster."

Justin's blue eyes kindled at the insult to both him and the young woman; his strong jaw clenched, but he kept his temper and resisted the impulse to tear into her. Wordlessly, he looked past her as if she did not exist and walked unhurriedly toward the card room.

With satisfaction, he heard Lady Willmer sputter behind him, "Well, I never . . ." at his suspect manners, which he had been afraid might have been lost on her. Ah, even petty revenge could sometimes be very sweet, he thought, as he nodded amiably to men and women whom he had not seen since his father's suicide.

* * *

From a far corner of the crowded card room, Henry Chasen smiled at Justin and waved him over to his table and to a chair opposite to him.

There was no awkwardness after years of separation between the two men, who had once been closer than brothers. From the letters exchanged over the years between Henry in England and Justin in the Far East, Justin knew his friend had been married for eight years and was the father of a son and daughter and that Arlene, his wife, was awaiting the birth of a third child.

Although Henry had intended to introduce Arlene to Justin this evening here at the assembly, his plans had gone awry when she became indisposed at the last minute. He had come to the dance alone and was now explaining this circumstance to Justin. "Had I known Arlene would not be with me, I would have had us meet somewhere else and not subject you to the gawking of these gapeseeds."

Justin expressed his regret that Henry's wife was ill, but said, "My presence here tonight serves a purpose. It will satisfy the curiosity of half the population of Carnbury Village, for it seems I am a nine days' wonder. But even nine days' wonders last only . . . well, nine days."

Both men laughed at Justin's inanity. "You are our first ever nabob," Henry pointed out, "and rather an oddity."

"I suppose I do look rather exotic with my dark skin and sun-streaked hair," Justin acknowledged.

"You at least have hair, and it is as thick and brown as when you left a dozen years ago," Henry said, running his fingers through his own thinning fair locks, but it was obvious he had something more important on his mind. His aspect became increasingly graver.

"I was pleased to learn you were able to regain

Sinclair Hall and some of your other properties that your father lost to Lord Dekker. But not the London town house, I hear."

"That was by design, Henry. I didn't even try to buy the place back. It would be too painful to live where my father took his life."

A waiter placed two glasses of a pale yellow liquid in front of the two gentlemen and left.

"Lemonade," Henry said, wrinkling his long nose. "It's warm." He pushed the glass away from him and studied Justin's dark face. "Rumors persist to this day that Lord Dekker cheated at cards." He looked for signs of bitterness in the earl's bright blue eyes, but saw none. Henry was not sure he himself would not have been soured for a lifetime had he been driven as a penniless lad from his ancestral home by his father's financial ruin.

Justin regarded Henry thoughtfully over the rim of his glass. "Lord Dekker is gone. Anger against a dead man is futile." He took a sip of the lemonade and grimaced.

"I knew you wouldn't like it," Henry said with a laugh.

Justin, too, shoved his glass aside. "Lord Dekker is ancient history, Henry."

On that note, the subject was closed. The years melted away in a swarm of recollections which began with childhood memories and segued into youthful escapades, which gave full rein to their mirth.

As the two old friends relived their many past larks and scrapes, the names Hobie, Dick, and Masters came up over and over again.

While in London, Justin had visited with those three gentlemen of the *ton*, who, along with Henry, were lifelong friends.

"I have invited Hobie, Dick, and Masters to the lodge for a fortnight of hunting in the new year and all have accepted. You will join us, of course," he said.

"I wouldn't miss it for the world," Henry replied. The hunting lodge was practically on his doorstep, so he would be able to take part in the reunion and still keep an eye on Arlene, who was going through a difficult pregnancy.

The turn in the conversation caused Justin to bring up the time he had stolen the keys to the lodge from his father's office. Henry laughed with him. The five friends had sown some of their wild oats that day, drinking immoderately and carousing with local wenches.

In passing, Henry mentioned the house was presently rented, but Justin treated the matter lightly. "Alvin Bodkin, who bought Sinclair Hall from Dekker, leased it to a Mrs. Barrow," he said, "but I will have regained the building by the first of the year."

Henry might have asked Justin more about his surprising statement, for he had not heard that Phoebe Barrow, with whom he was acquainted, was moving, but Justin was going on with his plans and the moment was lost.

"I have also extended invitations to friends from the English community in India who now reside in England to go hunting in February," Justin said. Hiding a smile, he added, "Oh, yes—I am entertaining the Prince Regent and his entourage at the lodge later that month."

He grinned at Henry's flabbergasted expression.

"How did you and George become so chummy?" Henry asked, his gray eyes wide.

Justin explained, "I was entrusted with a personal message to the Prince from a government official in India. George received me in private, and after our formal business was completed, he asked about my estate, sensible of the fact that this part of the country is renowned for hunting. Without going into chapter and verse, I invited him to be my guest, never dreaming he would accept."

"Gad Zeus, he really intends to come?"

Justin inclined his head. "Prince George was so delighted to be asked that he immediately called in his secretary and had him ink in the proposed date in his appointment book."

Henry was still shaking his head in wonder when he removed his pocket watch and snapped open the lid. "I could talk with you all night long, Justin, but Arlene doesn't close her eyes until I am safely home. This lying in has not gone as smoothly as with the first two children. Come by at your leisure any time. You will find me working somewhere on the property."

Justin issued a similar informal invitation to Sinclair Hall, which he explained was still mostly unfurnished. "But we can sit in the kitchen and talk," he said.

Once back in the ballroom, Justin asked Henry about the young woman called Dinah.

"Interested, eh?" Henry said with a gleam in his eyes. "She is quite pretty."

Justin smiled. "Yes she is, but it is just that I do not remember her from the old days."

Henry took him at his word and said, "Her full name is Dinah Monroe." He told Justin that Miss Monroe's father had been the pastor of St. Basil's for six years until his death the previous year. "Dinah was left without even a frugal monetary bequest, just a pile of old books. She works for Lady Willmer in different capacities, but lives with Mrs. Barrow and her orphans in your hunting lodge. Tonight she is earning a few coins by fetching for Lady Willmer, since the baroness's legs are bad."

Henry left then. A few minutes later, Justin, too, climbed into his carriage, still thinking about Miss Monroe. For some reason she intrigued him. He supposed he was experiencing one of those instant attractions he had heard about that sometimes happened between a man and a woman, but which until this evening he had not believed.

Henry had said Miss Monroe lived in the lodge with the war widow whose husband had fallen at Waterloo. He was aware of the orphans, but this was the first he had heard an adult other than Mrs. Phoebe Barrow resided in his property.

Fortunately, Alvin Bodkin had written the lease with a loophole clause. Justin would be able to reclaim the lodge from Mrs. Barrow before the hunting season. He rather hoped, though, that Miss Monroe would not resettle a great distance from Carnbury Village, for he had a real desire to become better acquainted with her.

Chapter 2

When Dinah came through the gate from the hunting lodge's back garden, she saw Lord Rushmore on horseback riding down the front drive toward the road. She decided he must have been making a neighborly call on Phoebe. She had an urge to choke Lady Willmer, who had kept her cooling her heels while she went over every item several times on the bill Dinah had rendered for her services.

Because of the difficult old woman's miserliness, she had missed a visit from the most exciting person to move to Carnbury Village in the seven years she had lived here. What bad luck!

Dinah watched the earl with bone-warming admiration. Last night he had flirted with her openly. She was flattered, but did not take his marked attention to heart. After all, a harmless flirtation was a hallmark of a gentleman of his class. But, undeniably, the earl's amusing regard had added a bit of sparkle to an otherwise dull evening.

Not until Lord Rushmore had reached a bend in the

drive and ridden out of Dinah's sight did she turn and walk up the steps of the weathered stone hunting lodge. Once inside, she divested herself of her drab bonnet and kerseymere cape in the vestibule and went to the main room, which always reminded her of a medieval hall in an ancient castle, with its high beamed ceilings and enormous stone fireplace. The room was divided into living and dining areas, which were capacious and commodious and designed to accommodate a houseful of sportsmen.

Phoebe was crumpled on the cushions of a sofa, her head in her hands. Alarmed, Dinah hurried to Phoebe, dropped down beside her, and wrapped her arms around her friend's sagging shoulders.

"What is wrong?" she asked, peering anxiously into the small oval face.

Phoebe pointed to the decanter of Madeira and a half-full wine glass on the tea table, as if the inanimate objects supplied the answer. "Lord Rushmore was here," she said on a sob. "We must move by the first of the year. His lordship has plans for the lodge."

Dinah removed her hands from the shoulders of the thirty-four-year-old woman who was eleven years her senior and frowned. "Your lease runs until June, Phoebe. The earl cannot put us out in January. You must have gotten something wrong."

Phoebe pulled a large handkerchief from the pocket of her plain blue dress and blew her nose. She pushed the cotton square back into her pocket and shook her head.

"No, I did not."

"What exactly did he say?" Dinah asked, her frown deepening.

Phoebe swallowed hard before she spoke. "He asked to see my copy of the lease, but I told him Mr. Bodkin kept the papers I signed. Whereupon he drew a document from his coat pocket and asked if that was my signature at the bottom."

"And was it?"

"Yes, but I never paid any mind to a clause which said that if the estate was sold, the new owner had the right to renegotiate the terms. How was I to know three years ago that Mr. Bodkin would sell out?" she wailed.

Her eyes on Phoebe's face, Dinah said, "Are you saying that Lord Rushmore can break the agreement you made with Alvin Bodkin?"

Phoebe looked unsure. "I think so," she said, her voice tentative, but calmer now that she could share her troubles with Dinah. "I was rendered speechless when he announced I must vacate the property by the first week in January. He said he would return the rent I paid for the months of November and December to compensate me for my inconvenience. But I don't want the earl's money. I just want to stay here."

"Even if you did want his money," Dinah said, "two months' rent is a mere pittance to a nabob. When you took over the lodge, it had been unoccupied for years and in a rundown condition. We slaved for over a week to make the place livable. He would be reaping the benefit of all our hard work."

Dinah's clergyman father had been alive when Phoebe moved into the building with her four orphans. As a charitable service of the church, Dinah had worked alongside Phoebe washing down the walls, cleaning the windows, removing the cobwebs, and polishing the ancient furniture. She and Phoebe had hauled the mattresses, which smelled musty from disuse, outdoors to air and had scraped the rust from the old iron stove and polished the metal until it shone like new.

But going off on a tangent was not going to get to

the truth, Dinah thought. Something wasn't right. She put a gentle hand on Phoebe's arm.

"Phoebe," she said, "if the lease you signed says you must renegotiate the terms with a new owner, common sense tells me Lord Rushmore cannot simply evict you unless you agree. You didn't agree, did you?"

Phoebe took a bracing breath. "I was too intimidated to disagree. The earl is a very forceful man."

"But you did not sign anything?"

"No. I simply nodded when he asked me if I understood what he was saying. He did not stay long. As you can see, he never even finished his wine."

Dinah did not want to believe it, yet it appeared Lord Rushmore might be taking advantage of Phoebe. Her friend tended to be meek and compliant when dealing with authority figures, but Dinah herself was not one to tremble at an aristocrat's displeasure and would have gotten to the truth. Lady Willmer had tried to cower her, but the baroness had soon found if she hoped to have Dinah as an employee, she would have to abide by Dinah's rules. Tyrants could take advantage only of those who allowed it. For now, she would give the earl the benefit of the doubt, but a plan was forming in her brain.

Dinah knew Phoebe loved the solid stone house, the secluded grounds, and the country location. Often her friend had said she had found the perfect place to raise her four orphans. Dinah felt she owed Phoebe a great deal. Perhaps this was the opportunity she had been looking for to repay her. She would do anything in her power to help Phoebe keep the lodge.

Dinah picked up Phoebe's work-worn hand and squeezed it.

"Give me your permission to speak to Lord Rushmore on your behalf, Phoebe. You seem very fuzzy about exactly what you did or did not agree to. Let me help."

Dinah's offer worked like a balm on Phoebe's shattered nerves. "Oh, would you please talk to his lordship, dear? I do so want to keep my home," she said. "I don't want the earl's money. I just want to remain his tenant, as I was to Alvin Bodkin. Mr. Bodkin wasn't the kindliest of men, but at least he left me alone."

"Leave it to me," Dinah said, as her natural optimism came to the fore. She could not imagine the charming gentleman with whom she had carried on a light flirtation was actually a villain in disguise. Trusting her instincts, she said, "I will get it straightened out. Now, let us put the problem with Lord Rushmore aside and go on to more pleasant matters."

Dinah pulled a pound note from the pocket of her high-necked dress. "Lady Willmer paid me today for my past two months' work. I plan to use part of the money for a Christmas celebration for the children," she said, brandishing the bill.

Phoebe welcomed the change of subject. "All right, tell me your scheme, for it is bound to be grand, if I know you."

Dinah giggled. "Not so grand—although perhaps a bit odd by English standards. Listen, Phoebe, I read the most interesting account of Christmas customs in America in a lady's periodical at Lady Willmer's. Do you know that in the state of Virginia the celebrations include fox hunts and firing guns in the air and enormous feasts on Christmas day?"

Phoebe looked suspicious. "You are not thinking of emulating the Virginians?"

"Gracious, no. But there was a reference to a writer called Washington Irving who wrote of Dutch Christmas traditions which had crossed the Atlantic. The

Dutch told their children Saint Nicholas flew over the trees in a wagon and dropped goodies down the chimney into stockings hung on the fireplace."

Now it was Phoebe's turn to giggle. "What hogwash! However would this saint get the horses to leap so high?"

Dinah laughed. "Don't be silly. It is merely a Banbury tale for poppets." Phoebe laughed with her, then raised a brow.

"St. Nicholas? What could he possibly have to do with Christmas? What did he look like?"

Dinah shrugged. "I have no idea. The dissertation was not illustrated."

"The gifts would burn to a crisp in the fire," Phoebe said, playing along as if she believed the tale.

"They landed in the stockings by magic," Dinah chimed in. The two women burst into uncontrolled laughter at the absurdities.

When sanity returned, Dinah said, "The children will love it," and Phoebe agreed.

Dinah went on. "I intend to make each of them a wide stocking-shaped receptacle from red felt, in which we can put their Christmas orange and sugarplums and nuts."

"At least that sounds doable," Phoebe granted.

"But the part of the New Yorkers' festivities—for that is where the Dutch settled—which I want to be the main event in our celebration will be baking cookies. In the article, the writer said Saint Nicholas crossed the ocean and brought all kinds of cookies with him from Holland."

Phoebe pulled a face. "I assume he came by ship this time, instead of his flying wagon. Cookies are sweet biscuits, aren't they?"

"Yes. I believe the name comes from the Dutch word

for a little cake, *koekje*. We can bake some sort of jumbles as a family project, with everyone pitching in," Dinah said. "We will put together something easy enough for the children to make at little cost. We already have most of the ingredients and can manage to buy a bit of sugar and some nuts."

Dinah had been raised in the church, where the holiday was solemn and religious in nature. Thinking of this, Phoebe said, "I know all this jollity is a far cry from the memories of your Christmases in the rectory."

"Yes," Dinah replied, "but, you know, Phoebe, I would hear about the gaiety of London Christmases and some of our more affluent neighbors in my father's old parish kept the holiday, too. I envied them. I wanted to decorate the rectory with evergreen boughs and invite neighbors to partake of a bowl of mulled wine and sing carols."

Phoebe shook her head. "I fear your papa would have been shocked."

"I don't think he would have been, but I thought so at the time. So I never dared make the suggestion."

The outside door, which led from the garden into the kitchen, opened and slammed shut.

"The children are home," Phoebe said. Soon her brood of four orphans could be heard coming toward them from the back of the lodge, noisily talking over each other.

Dinah tucked the pound note back into her pocket and spoke in a low voice. "Let us not say anything to the children about moving." She had observed Lord Rushmore at the assembly. He had appeared confident, not arrogant, and friendly, not condescending—in a word, approachable. "I am certain I can iron out our differences with the earl," she said and gave Phoebe a reassuring hug.

Chapter 3

Justin filled a copper teakettle with water from the kitchen pump, which Alvin Bodkin had installed in Sinclair Hall during his tenure. He placed the kettle on the iron stove in which he had built a fire earlier and leaned against the counter to wait for the water to boil.

His brain had seemed filled with mental pictures of Dinah Monroe ever since the dance. He wasn't sure why, for while she stood out in the country crowd for her prettiness, she would hardly cause a stir in Town.

Justin chuckled. The devil she wouldn't. Decked out in the kick of fashion instead of in that dated pink dress and sporting a fancy hairdo instead of that tidy casual topknot, she would have outshone the current toast by a league.

From a shelf behind the sink, Justin removed a china cup and saucer and a Blue Willow patterned teapot which he had purchased in a Bond Street shop. He set out the crockery on a wooden table beside a sugar bowl and a caddy of Earl Grey tea from Fortnum and Mason.

He was beguiled by the clergyman's daughter, no doubt of it. Yet marriage was too important to pick a wife on a whim. That he was even considering Dinah Monroe in that light amazed him, for he was not given to rash decisions. Miss Monroe was the first woman ever to whom he had been strongly attracted at first sight. What that meant, if anything, only time would tell.

The clang of the brass knocker on the front door sent Justin to remove the kettle from the fire and set it aside on an unheated part of the stove. He wondered who could be calling on him, since he had made it generally known he was not receiving visitors.

As he slid the bolt, it crossed his mind that the caller might be Henry Chasen. But when he jerked open the door, his heart skipped a beat. Dinah Monroe stood before him in a dark green day dress, looking as startled as he. Four redheaded children, dressed in country clothes appropriate for the mild fall day, stood behind her on the drive.

Dinah's heart fluttered like a trapped bird. She had expected a servant to respond to her knock, not the master of the house in his shirtsleeves. But her voice was calm when she said, "Good day, my lord. I am Dinah Monroe. I would like to have a word with you, if I may."

The earl smiled in a friendly manner, revealing straight teeth which appeared especially white against his tanned skin. "I am your servant, ma'am." He nodded his head in polite deference to her. "And I know your name."

Dinah raised a surprised brow. "We had a brief encounter at the assembly, but we were never introduced. In fact, my lord, I believe we did not exchange even a single word." *Only looks of ill-concealed curiosity.*

"True," he replied with complete candor, thinking much the same thoughts as she. "I got your name from Henry Chasen."

Dinah felt pleased that the earl had been interested enough in her to ask Henry her name. But with this sort of encouragement from a handsome lord, a girl could make a fool of herself. Not a wise path to follow.

Dinah pulled herself together and got down to business. "May the children visit the horses pastured near the barn?" she asked. "They saw the animals from the road. While they are so engaged, I would beg a private word with you, sir."

Justin consented cheerily to her request. He was curious to learn why she had sought him out, but was delighted she had, for her precipitating their meeting fell in quite nicely with his own desire to get to know her better. He walked down the steps with her and over to the children, whom he guessed correctly were the orphans under Mrs. Barrow's care.

Identical mops of flaming red hair covered the young heads; myriad freckles spread over the homey faces. No one would have called them pretty children, but there was something endearing in their lively open expressions. They stared at Justin as if he had come from the moon.

The two wide-eyed boys whispered to one another while an older girl stood with her rosebud lips slightly parted. A smaller girl had a thumb tucked firmly in her tiny mouth.

The taller boy said in a stage whisper to the others, "He's the nabob."

Sliding her thumb from her mouth, the smaller girl cocked her head like a tiny red bird and said, "Hullo, Nabob."

"He is a lord, silly," the older girl reprimanded her sister.

"Oh, hullo, Lord Nabob," the child amended solemnly.

"No, Lily." Miss Monroe put a gentle hand on the child's shoulder. "This is Lord Rushmore."

Lily's hands went to her hips. She scowled fiercely and stamped her small black-booted foot. "What *is* your name?" she said, frustrated.

The earl laughed. "Justin," he replied. "And yours, I deduce, is Lily."

"Lord Rushmore!" Miss Monroe cried, "do not encourage the child in a display of raggedy manners. She will start calling you by your given name. Lily, the gentleman's proper form of address is Lord Rushmore."

Justin rolled his eyes to the sky, which set the child giggling.

"I like Lord Nabob better," Lily said, emboldened by his compatibility.

The older girl took a step forward to position herself closer to Justin and acted as the spokesperson for the group. In a grown-up voice, she said, "We are the Connors. I'm Martha. And this is Sidney," she pointed over her shoulder toward the taller boy. "He is ten. Malcolm is eight. I am eleven, and Lily is only five, which is why she is so confused."

"Thank you for introducing everyone so properly, Miss Martha." Justin smiled down at her. "You have exceedingly fine manners."

Martha's answering smile was rendered smugly superior by the compliment.

"What is a nabob exactly?" Malcolm asked, now that he was no longer awestruck by the dark stranger, who had shown himself to be totally harmless and quite friendly.

Sidney spoke up. "It is what an English gentleman who has made a fortune in India is called. At least that is what Mr. Chasen told me," he said. "He is our neighbor," he explained, looking up at Justin.

"Yes, I know him," Justin said.

To Dinah it seemed rude to be drawing attention to his lordship's stupendous wealth with the gentleman himself present. "May the children go to see the horses now, my lord?" she asked, to divert any further discussion of the monetary status of nabobs.

"Why don't we all go?" the earl suggested. "I shall speak with Mr. O'Shay, my groom, and ask him to give the children horseback rides in the ring. Would you like that?" His encompassing glance took in all of the carrot-topped youngsters. Not unexpectedly, he was met with an excited chorus of affirmatives to the promised treat.

The earl pointed them in the direction of the path to the stable, which was hidden behind a grove of trees, many of which still had their fall leaves of red and gold. The children ran ahead as Dinah and his lordship followed, speaking of nothing more significant than the splendid weather.

The earl quickly settled the matter of the youngsters' rides with Mr. O'Shay, his newly hired groom, and a seventeen-year-old stable boy, Sammy. Both were locals and well known to Dinah and the children, who greeted them by name.

A hound puppy ambled from the stables, drawn from her nap by the human voices, and lazily stretched her hind legs behind her.

"A doggie," Lily cried and knelt down in the grass. The brown and white dog proceeded to lick her hand.

"What is the doggie's name, Lord Nabob?" Lily asked.

Dinah cringed at the appellation, but the earl seemed undisturbed by the indecorous title.

"She has not been named yet, Lily. I bought her only yesterday from the blacksmith in the village."

"She should be called Dulcie," the little girl said, decisively.

The earl shrugged. "Why not? Dulcie, she is. Mr. O'Shay?" He looked at his head groom for confirmation.

"A fine name," Mr. O'Shay said, patting Lily's head. Malcolm and Sidney joined their younger sister on the grass and petted the hound. It wriggled excitedly in doggie bliss from all the unexpected human attention. Ladylike, Martha stood apart watching her siblings.

Justin took the opportunity to invite Miss Monroe to the house for a cup of tea. "We can talk there uninterrupted."

Assured that Mr. O'Shay and Sammy would look after the children, Dinah agreed. She explained where she would be to the Connors.

"Come to the hall when you have had your rides and wait for me on the front steps," she instructed them.

In the manor kitchen, the earl put the kettle back onto the burner. "The water will come to a boil in a minute." He lifted a stove lid and fed in another chunk of wood.

Dinah sat down at the spotless table where the earl was adding a second cup and saucer and two dessert plates to the dishes already there.

"You have no servants," she observed. She had never heard of a lord of the realm doing for himself.

"I will hire household staff eventually. But for now, I can take care of my own needs. It hasn't been too many years since I have been able to afford to hire a full complement of servants," he said, breaking into a winning smile. "Even now, I get along without a valet, but I don't let it get around, for I fear it will lower me in the eyes of my peers."

Dinah smiled at the self-effacing confession.

"But fear not, Miss Monroe, I can brew an adequate pot of tea," he said, winking at her.

She had to laugh. Lord Rushmore had none of the arrogance she had found an integral part of the makeup of the few aristocrats she had met. A woman could easily give her heart to such a man. But she was so far beneath him socially, it would be a decidedly one-sided affair. Titled gentlemen who were rich and handsome did not marry clergymen's daughters. Anyway, the whole idea was absurd.

Dinah watched him remove the kettle from the stove, wrapping a pot holder around the handle. With strong, capable hands, he poured the boiling water over the tea leaves in the Spode teapot. He went to the pantry and returned with a plate of cinnamon buns. "I baked these this morning," he said, a twinkle in his bright blue eyes.

"How clever of you," Dinah replied, tongue-in-cheek, for she had identified the pastries as a specialty of the village bake shop.

The earl took two napkins from a kitchen drawer, handed one to Dinah, and sat down across from her, putting the other napkin beside his dessert plate. As they waited for the tea to steep, she asked him, "When do you expect to have the hall furnished?" She had noticed the other rooms they passed on the way to the kitchen were empty.

When Dinah had first come to Carnbury Village, she had heard that Lord Dekker, the old earl's creditor, had auctioned off the original furnishings of Sinclair Hall. She herself had seen the train of wagons two months ago which Alvin Bodkin, the subsequent owner, had used to move his possessions to his new home in a distant town.

The earl raised his broad shoulders in a shrug at her question. "I have bought a few essential pieces like this kitchen table and the chairs, and, of course, a bed, a washstand, and a comfortable fireside chair for the room in which I sleep. The chamber is the one I occupied as a boy, but I am leaving the major purchases and the decorating to my wife," he informed her.

A puzzled frown creased Dinah's forehead. "I had not heard that you are married, my lord," she said.

"I'm not. But I plan to be."

Dinah rummaged up a lukewarm smile. "Congratulations," she said, not examining why her heart dropped. "Who is the fortunate lady?"

"No one as yet," he said, "but I am actively seeking a wife. I believe that is the phraseology in common use."

Dinah knew her relief was completely irrational. She certainly was not in the running, but she thought she might like to be.

The earl poured their tea into the china cups and passed Dinah hers. He took a bite from the cinnamon bun and chewed carefully, all the while looking at Dinah with interest.

"Henry Chasen said your late father served at St. Basil's. I was baptized in that church."

Dinah was curious about him and he was curious about her, which made it easy to speak effortlessly with him.

"Papa was not particularly successful in his vocation, as you have probably surmised, since he was serving in a village church in middle age." She added sugar to her tea and took a sip. "You do know how to brew an excellent pot of tea, my lord."

He smiled his thanks and Dinah went on, "Papa was not sufficiently dedicated to his preaching. He cared more about his scholarly pursuits than about writing sermons or inspiring his congregation with fresh material. In fact, he never bothered to write a new sermon after his first year in the ministry."

Lord Rushmore chuckled. "You are exaggerating."

Smiling, Dinah shook her head. "I still have in my possession the twelve months of Sunday homilies which he recirculated year after year."

"The reverend sounds like a resourceful fellow," the earl said, draining his cup and setting it onto its matching saucer.

"I suppose one could look at it that way," Dinah said. "In any case, he was a good man. Rarely did he have an unkind word to say about anyone. He simply lacked worldly ambitions, but I am certain he was happier for it."

But Dinah had not forgotten her reason for requesting this interview and now said, "I wish to speak with you, my lord, about your determination to evict Mrs. Barrow from the hunting lodge."

The earl arched a brow. "*Evict* is such a harsh word, Miss Monroe. I am simply renegotiating the lease, as is my right by the terms of Mrs. Barrow's agreement with Alvin Bodkin."

"Where is the negotiation, my lord? You dictated the terms to Mrs. Barrow."

Justin was surprised by her critical attack. "Mrs. Barrow agreed," he said in his defense. "I am compensating her for her inconvenience by giving her two months' free rent. The money will be in her hands by the end of the week."

"You intimidated Phoebe Barrow. She did not know how to deal with you."

A red flag went up in Justin's brain. Miss Monroe, it seemed, was not going to be accommodating. But what business was this of hers? He leaned back in his chair. "You wrong me, ma'am. I am not so badly behaved as to intimidate a lady."

"Perhaps not intentionally," she conceded. "In any case, Mrs. Barrow intends to remain at the lodge until June, when her lease runs out. What she would like to negotiate is an agreement to extend the lease past this summer."

Justin shook his head slowly from side to side. "Out of the question, Miss Monroe." He leaned his arms on the table. "How do you figure in this anyway? Mrs. Barrow's name is the one on the agreements, not yours."

Dinah squared her shoulders and stated flatly, "I am acting as Phoebe Barrow's agent."

"Her agent? Since when has the occupation been open to women?" He brushed aside his own question with a wave of his hand, for Miss Monroe looked even more unaccommodating. He did not like it, but he decided to go along with her charade.

"All right, Agent," he said, with a hint of mockery, "let's negotiate. If two months' rent is not enough compensation to be out of the lodge by the first week in January, how much is?" Money was always a successful inducement in Justin's world.

Dinah sighed deeply. "You don't seem to understand, sir. Mrs. Barrow likes the house very much. She does not want to move at all."

Justin stroked his chin and narrowed his eyes. Getting out of this lease was going to cost him more than he had expected. But his investments mushroomed daily. He could afford to pay whatever it took to get the lodge back. He would sweeten the pot with an offer which would be impossible for her to refuse.

"If Mrs. Barrow will vacate the premises by the first of the year, I will pay her the cash equivalent of the six months of rent left on her lease."

But Justin found Miss Monroe's face did not soar with elation as he had expected. She frowned and said, "Why are you so anxious to get rid of Phoebe?"

"Dash it all, Miss Monroe," he said, "I do not have a personal vendetta against your friend. The south of England is popular for hunting during January and February because of our mild weather. While sojourning in London recently, I invited a good number of very close friends to be my guests during the coming season. I also have particular weeks spoken for by gentlemen I knew in business in India. Moreover, Prince George plans to come for a number of days."

"Prince George? The Regent?" Dinah was amazed.

"The same," the earl said. "You see how impossible it will be for Mrs. Barrow to remain as my tenant. I did not know Alvin Bodkin had leased the lodge when I invited these gentlemen."

Dinah pursed her lips. She was not callous to his dilemma. Prince George! My goodness! "Why can't you house your guests here in the hall?" she suggested.

"Out of the question," the earl said. "The wallpaper has to be replaced and carpets installed. All manner of household goods from kitchen pans to sofas and beds to linens have to be purchased, not to mention hiring a trained staff of servants. Making the hall livable will require months of preparation. The lodge can be made ready for a party of gentlemen in a matter of days."

"The lodge is in such excellent condition due to

Phoebe's care. Mr. Bodkin required her to make repairs and pay for all the upkeep," Dinah pointed out.

"For a greatly reduced rent, I believe," the earl countered.

"My lord, Mr. Bodkin tried to lease the building for hunting, but no one wanted the lodge. Phoebe needed a large house, but lived on a small pension. Mr. Bodkin let her have it rather than have the building stay empty. But she had to put a lot of work into making the lodge habitable."

The earl pushed away from the table as if ending the negotiations. "Draw up a bill for those repairs which covers all of Mrs. Barrow's outlays during her years of occupancy. Now, is there anything else?"

Dinah disentwined her fingers from the handle of her teacup and pushed it aside. "You still do not understand. This is not about money, my lord. Phoebe does not want to move."

"Well, she will have to," he said, showing his expasperation openly for the first time. "I have been exceedingly generous in meeting Mrs. Barrow's concerns. As her agent, you are responsible for taking my terms back to her."

Justin reminded himself that though Miss Monroe was proving to be a more formidable opponent than the shy Mrs. Barrow, it was the widow's name that was on the legal papers. "I cannot imagine Mrs. Barrow will turn down such an advantageous offer," he said.

Dinah could see she was not going to change Lord Rushmore's mind today. She would have to retreat for now and rethink her strategies. She extended her hand across the table. "I shall carry your offer to my client," she said, remaining carefully expressionless and businesslike.

Justin wrapped his strong fingers around Miss Monroe's small hand and gave her a soft look. "Believe me, ma'am, I do not want to cause Mrs. Barrow undue distress. But the lodge is rightfully mine to do with as I please. It was never meant to be a family home." He smiled charmingly. "I tell you what, I will make an estate agent available at my expense to assist Mrs. Barrow in finding another home that is to her liking."

Dinah removed her hand from his. The earl obviously believed money was the answer to every problem. And from what she had heard, he had tons of it. She got up. "Thank you for the tea, Lord Rushmore," she said, ignoring his last concession.

Justin noticed, but did not take offense. He rather liked her spirit. She had presented the widow's case as intelligently as any man would have. He had no intention of giving in to her demands, yet she had done nothing to kill his desire to get to know her better.

He stood up with her. "I would like very much for us to become friends, Miss Monroe," he said, deciding to speak plainly and not mince words. "Pray do not let our differences on this particular matter stand in the way of that goal."

Dinah was too aware of the failure of her mission to pay attention to his olive branch. She had given Phoebe hope and must now dash it—or at least temper it. She walked to the front door more quickly than usual. The earl followed and opened it for her, but did not go beyond the threshold.

Before she ascended the steps to the drive where the Connors were waiting, Dinah remembered to ask the earl to thank Mr. O'Shay and Sammy on her behalf for taking care of the children.

Justin nodded and held up his hand in farewell to

the youngsters, who followed Martha's example and shouted their own thanks for the horseback rides.

"Come again soon," Justin said in reply.

"Tomorrow, Lord Nabob?" Sidney asked with a grin.

Miss Monroe chided the boy for his impertinence, but Justin replied, "Every day, if you like, Sidney. The horses can use the exercise." He sighed and turned back into the house.

Chapter 4

Dinah pinned up the bottoms of the valance from around her bed and swept the floor underneath while Phoebe unlooped the curtains from the upstairs window and shook them out. They were wearing their oldest clothes while doing the heavy cleaning.

Clutching the curtains to her breast, Phoebe said, "I keep telling myself I should not have such an illogical attachment to the lodge, but all my life I followed the drum. Captain Barrow and I never had a permanent home, nor were we blessed with children. The very thought of being uprooted from here makes me dejected and my heart sad."

Dinah replaced the valance around the bed and smoothed the bedcovers. She emptied the contents of the dustpan into a trash bin and propped her broom against the wall.

"Let's rest a minute, Phoebe," Dinah said as she sat down on the edge of the bed.

Phoebe descended from the step stool, which she

had used to rehang the window curtains, and dropped into a Windsor chair.

"Am I wrong, Dinah, for not being swayed by the earl's generous terms? For they are generous, you know. It would give us a measure of security if we added that money to our coffers."

She tucked a stray lock of brown hair back under her mob cap as she looked at Dinah, who sat across from her, saying nothing. "You think me a silly woman, don't you?"

"No, dear, no, no. I do not." Dinah vaulted from the bed and knelt down before Phoebe on the multicolored hooked rug, her hands on her friend's knees. She felt a rush of love for this unselfish, kindhearted woman.

"What would I have done if you had not offered me a home when my dear papa died? I might have had no choice but to live with Lady Willmer and put up with her cantankerousness every day. I owe you so much." Dinah sat back on her heels. "We are not going to bend to Lord Rushmore's will, no matter how much money he dangles to try to seduce us. I have been thinking of something he said when I left him yesterday. He wants me to be his friend."

Phoebe looked at her in a peculiar fashion. "Friend? You mean he is not indifferent to you in a *special* way? He wants to court you?"

Dinah sat down cross-legged on the rug at Phoebe's feet. "No, nothing like that," she said, being careful not to give away her own interest in the earl. "After all, he must look much higher than a poor clergyman's daughter for a wife. Henry Chasen told me Lord Rushmore wants nothing so much as to start a family to restore his aristocratic line. He would need a nobleman's daughter for that."

"Then what?" Phoebe asked.

"Lord Rushmore has invited the children to come to the hall to ride the horses whenever they want. You heard how excited they were when they told you of their visit. We will take advantage of his invitation, for I am sure he is sincere."

Phoebe frowned. "I am afraid I do not see what you are driving at. How will this help our cause?"

"I don't think the idea of my being your agent was a good one. I need an excuse to go to Sinclair Hall that has nothing to do with the lodge, a neighborly sort of thing. I cannot change Lord Rushmore's mind if I never have polite discourse with him. I hope when he gets to know me better, he will be more receptive to extending the lease."

"But it was Mr. O'Shay and Sammy who gave the children their rides. Will the earl put in an appearance?"

Dinah got up and picked up her broom. "I think so." The earl had definitely said he wanted them to be friends. She could only hope he had not changed his mind.

Dinah had nothing to worry about. Had she not shown up the next day at his estate, Justin would have found an excuse to further their acquaintance by calling at the lodge.

But her initiative took a worrisome burden from his shoulders. If she failed to suit, he could save face by withdrawing without seeming to reject her.

The ensuing days for both of them fell into a rhythm. While the children were occupied horseback riding under Mr. O'Shay's keen eye, Dinah and the earl, content with each other's company, strolled through the grounds, where even in December a few flowers bloomed.

They talked and talked and talked about their personal lives, about art, about music, about everything. Although Dinah had led a restricted life, she read widely. The information she had garnered from books, periodicals, and newspapers made her knowledgeable on a wide range of subjects.

However, every time she decided to broach the subject of the lodge on Phoebe's behalf, her heart balked at inserting a sour note into her harmonious dialogue with the earl.

A few days before Christmas, she knew she could no longer put off what had become an unwelcome task. She strolled arm in arm with the earl toward the stables under the clear blue skies, intending to confront him. But she was finding it difficult. Instead, she talked about her Christmas plans.

"Why a Christmas based on some American custom?" the earl asked her after she had told him about the article in the periodical. "Why not stick with the English holiday . . . a Yule log, wassail bowl, and mistletoe?"

"The English traditions seem more in keeping with an adult celebration," she explained. "I want something different for the children. Eggnog is more appropriate for them than wassail, and Sidney and the rest would turn up their noses at a kissing ball. Baking sweet biscuits will be much more fun than watching a Yule log burn. Henry Chasen is bringing us oranges from London for the stockings I made."

"At least oranges are traditional fare for giving to English children at Christmas," he said. "How about comfits and sugarplums and nuts?"

"Oh, yes, Phoebe and I plan to fill the Dutch stockings with the usual goodies." Phoebe's name triggered Dinah's guilt.

Suddenly she stopped beneath the towering trees of the grove, turned to him, and blurted out, "Phoebe is quite heartbroken, my lord. Won't you please reconsider and let her remain as your tenant at the lodge?"

Justin dropped Dinah's arm as if he had been burned. "Where did that come from? We were speaking about Christmas."

Just this morning he had hired an estate agent to find a suitable house for Mrs. Barrow, at considerable expense to himself. "I thought the matter of the lodge was settled," he said, his eyes flashing blue fire. "I have a stack of acceptances for the upcoming hunting season piled on my kitchen table, including an enthusiastic reply from the Prince Regent." He crossed his arms over his chest defiantly. "Exactly what is so wonderful about the lodge that Mrs. Barrow continues to lament leaving it?"

Given his mocking tone, Dinah knew her words of explanation would be useless, even before she spoke them. "A hundred little things. I can't put it into words. It's a feeling. Sometimes, my lord, something is just perfect."

"Ridiculous," the earl muttered. "Women, I fear, are inept when it comes to business. Alvin Bodkin gloried at the handsome profit I offered him for Sinclair Hall. Mrs. Barrow would do well to consider the money instead of feelings."

Dinah watched him walk away from her in what she termed a snit, which made further pleas impossible. She knew she would never convince him one could not put a price on everything. How could she, when the fortune he had earned had made it possible for him to buy back everything his father had lost?

Dinah went to collect the children. She stood a little apart from the earl, who was leaning on the fence watching Mr. O'Shay as he instructed the two boys in mounting and dismounting properly. On a horse called Pansy, Martha sat on a woman's saddle, which Mr. O'Shay had purchased from a secondhand dealer, her skirts pulled down very properly to her ankles. Outside the fence, Lily played nearby on the grass with the little hound dog.

"From which parent did the children inherit their red hair?" Lord Rushmore asked Dinah.

She embraced the casual remark, relieved that the indignation had drained from his eyes. "According to Phoebe, both Sergeant Connor and his wife were redheads from Irish stock," she said.

Justin knew the children had been on the continent during the Battle of Waterloo. Mrs. Barrow had nursed their consumptive mother in her last days. Ironically, Mrs. Connor had passed away the same day as her husband was killed in the fighting.

"Captain Barrow died in the same battle as the children's father, didn't he?" Justin said.

"Yes," Dinah replied. "Sergeant Connor had been a member of Captain Barrow's company. When the captain did not come home after the battle, Phoebe prayed her husband was still alive, for chaos reigned after the fighting stopped. But she finally got word both the captain and the sergeant had fallen. Phoebe could not bring herself to consign the Connor children to an orphanage, so she adopted them."

For some reason, her words made Justin feel like a scoundrel, but he found the impression absurd. He had nothing to do with Napoleon's war.

He unlatched the paddock gate, since the three older children were done riding. Worn out from running after Dulcie, Lily declined Mr. O'Shay's offer of a pony ride.

The groom kenneled the dog to keep the devoted hound from following Lily home. Dinah thanked him for his kind attention to Sidney, Malcolm, and Martha.

Justin waited until the children had run a few yards ahead of them on the path to the hall before he put a firm hand on Dinah's arm and stopped her.

"Come horseback riding with me tomorrow," he said. The decision was not as sudden as it sounded. "You do ride?"

Dinah's brown eyes shimmered with surprise, but she did not hesitate. "Yes," she said, "although I haven't in a very long time." A warmth seeped through her. It meant so much to her that the earl still wanted to be with her, for she had fallen in love with him. Happily, she said, "I assume you mean for us to ride without the children, my lord."

The earl let out a faint but unmistakable chuckle. "Definitely without the children."

"I would like that, if you promise I can ride Pansy. My skills are bound to be rusty," Dinah said. The mare Martha rode seemed gentle and easy to handle.

The earl agreed and settled on a time with her. "I shall bring Pansy, fully bridled and saddled, to the hunting lodge."

He took her elbow and continued toward the hall, where the children were sprawled on the stone steps.

Dinah made her farewell to the earl and gathered the children to her.

"Good-bye, Lord Nabob," Sidney called, and the others copied him. The earl, who had come to respond to the improper title as if it were his baptismal name, waved to them and sat down on the steps. He leaned back, his elbows on the step above. He looked out over his recovered heritage, content with what he had accomplished.

But unless he married, his family would end with him. All his acquisitions would be to no purpose.

Dinah Monroe was a special woman and seemed to be everything he was looking for in a mate. Only one detail needed to be resolved. Husbands and wives in some circles went their own ways, but Justin intended to be a faithful husband. Yet he had no intention of spending a lifetime married to a frigid woman. He wanted a bride who would set his blood on fire and who would respond to his lovemaking with unbridled passion. Tomorrow he would attempt to raise the sort of heat between him and Miss Monroe which could be quenched in only one way.

Chapter 5

Dinah sat down on the long log, which had been stripped of its branches, beside the brook. She sometimes brought the children here for a picnic.

The earl had settled back against a willow tree and was watching the horses drink from the crystal stream. Before they left the lodge, Justin had insisted they dispense with formalities and address each other by their given names. But his mood had changed almost as soon as he had helped her to dismount here at the brook from the new lady's saddle which he had bought for her, claiming Martha's was too small for an adult.

The weather was beautifully sunny and lovely for December. Dinah noticed Justin's bright blue eyes darted here and there, and his frown increased when the sound of a group of boys downstream became louder and drew closer. She wished he would be as gay as his dark red coat, which he wore over tan riding breeches tucked into dark brown riding boots, and would get rid of that expression, which resembled a thundercloud.

Justin kicked the grass at his feet with the toe of his fine leather boot. The tryst he had planned had to be aborted. He had remembered this meadow, where purple foxgloves bloomed all summer, as being off the beaten path. In fact, he and Henry had called it their secret place, since no one ever came here. Now it seemed to have turned into a favorite of the locals. A footpath ran along the brook, the dirt packed down from years of use.

"The brook here used to be deserted," he grumbled.

Dinah wore a forest green jacket and matching riding skirt, which she had remade from an old habit of Phoebe's. To her, Justin's annoyance seemed out of proportion to the situation. He had stopped here to water the horses and would be moving on in a few minutes, but she said, "There are more houses close by than there were a dozen years ago. Lady Willmer complains endlessly about the growing population, but then nothing pleases her."

"I know," Justin said. "She used to find pleasure in reminding me of my father's faults when I was just a lad— as though I was responsible for his profligate ways."

"You must have gotten back at her at the dance, for she called you an odious man, among other things," Dinah said.

Justin heard the smile in her voice. He smiled, too. "I did give her a rather pointed set down, but she deserved the censure." He did not tell Dinah the slight was as much for her as for himself. Instead he said, "How do you stand her?"

"She needs me," Dinah replied. "Finding someone in the country for hire who is adequately educated to perform the duties she requires is next to impossible. She has learned to be civil to me or lose my services." She shrugged. "As I have told you before, Justin, I need her, too. My earnings help with our household expenses."

Justin nodded, but his mind went back to the matter at hand. He could not make love to Dinah when a pack of unruly boys was bearing down on them. There must be someplace around here where he could steal an uninterrupted kiss and test her passion.

Justin's chestnut stallion, Jasper, and Pansy, the docile little mare, had come up from the brook and were cropping the grass on the embankment.

"Let us ride on," Justin said, anxious to be on his way in hopes of finding a likely spot for an assignation.

Justin was relatively quiet as they rode companionably over the gently rolling wooded hills, past hedgerows and granite boulders. Dinah did not mind his periods of silence, for he did turn an occasional soft smile on her. She liked being with Justin. Looking at him. He was so wholly, implicitly male. Life would be wonderful if he would fall in love with her, she thought.

Although Dinah had never been this far from the village before, Justin had explored the peaceful, still unspoiled land on horseback with Henry when they were boys.

Justin was sharing with Dinah one of the silly things that happened in those past years when they came upon an abandoned sheepherder's hut in a field of high grasses. Justin stopped, got down from Jasper, and wrapped the reins around a bush. Dinah slid from the lady's saddle and joined him in front of the derelict shack.

"The shepherd who lived here was called Silas," Justin said. "I wonder what became of him?" The place looked deserted.

"Most of the farmers today raise cattle and corn, not sheep," Dinah said, suggesting a reason as she looked at the adjacent pastures.

Justin couldn't have cared less about the district's farming practices. His heart was racing faster as his mind thought about the lustier activites which might now be possible.

The yard which circled the hut was overgrown and showed no evidence of human trespass. He looked over the surrounding countryside and saw no farmhouses or barns. There was nothing but undisturbed rural tranquility to the horizon.

Taking Dinah's hand, Justin said, "Let's have a look inside."

She resisted. "Deserted huts often harbor snakes or rats."

Justin grinned down at her. "I will leave the door open in the event we encounter crawling creatures and must make a hasty retreat."

"All right," she said, still hesitant.

Justin lifted the latch and pushed the door in. He dropped Dinah's hand and stepped into the single room, stamping his boots on the dirt floor. He cocked his head and listened for scuttling or slithering sounds, but he heard nothing, and nothing moved.

"It's safe," he said, handing Dinah into the hut.

Still leery, she stuck close to Justin's side as he moved further into the small musty room. The interior seemed dark after the bright sunshine, but her eyes quickly adjusted to the dimness. The hut contained a few pieces of broken furniture and an intact backless bench. One wall was taken up by a stone fireplace.

Justin went to the single window and opened the shutters, letting in more light.

He turned from the window and faced Dinah. She

looked directly into his intense blue eyes, and her legs went weak when he set his strong hands on her shoulders.

Justin felt Dinah tremble. "Don't be afraid, sweetheart," he said, his voice husky, but very gentle and tender. "I was quite bowled over by you when I first saw you at the assembly. My desire for you has only increased since then." He ran his palm down the soft glow of her cheeks and touched her mouth with his forefinger.

"I am going to kiss you, Dinah," he said, pulling her closer.

Dinah wound her arms around his neck even before he lowered his lips and pressed them against her now willing mouth. His kiss was long and deep and left her swamped with passion.

Justin kissed her again and again until the blood seemed to thunder in Dinah's ears. By the time his deft fingers began to unfasten the buttons of her jacket, her moral upbringing had fled completely, and she had lost the will to resist him. She moaned when his warm lips stole down the column of her exposed neck and lingered on the soft flesh at the top of her breasts.

Justin felt he would explode with the force of his need. Dinah had fired his blood into an unbelievable conflagration. But he had to stop. Come back to earth. It would be shoddy to take her in this abandoned shack.

Breathing hard, he held her at arm's length.

"Marry me, Dinah," he said.

Dinah's heart soared with happiness. Dreams did come true. Justin loved her. Unable to speak, she rose up on her toes, slid one hand behind his neck, pulled down his head, and kissed him warmly.

Delighted, Justin lifted his mouth from hers and laughed lightly. "I take it that is a yes." He pulled her down to sit beside him on Silas's wooden bench. Dinah had exceeded his wildest expectations. She was so sweet. So amorous. So unrestrained. So perfect!

He felt a little giddy. "Oh, sweetheart, you have just passed the final test for a wife. You've made me very happy."

The hut became quiet. Dinah slid over on the bench to where she could turn and face Justin. She thought he looked very puffed-up and smug. Her heart fell. "Final test?" she said.

Justin perceived his mistake immediately and swore under his breath.

"Don't get into a pelter, my dear," he said in an attempt to overcome his blunder. Dinah looked like she was ready to drag him over the coals. "I felt it was wiser to test our passions before we agreed to wed. I did not think it would be fair to you if you found my lovemaking objectionable."

Dinah's lip curled as she read his mind. He had twisted the truth to mend his gaffe. Turning his upside-down statement right side up, she said, "No, *you* did not want a wife who was cold and unresponsive. You were not even thinking of me."

Justin hated being exposed as less than honest and attempted to mitigate the damage with a slice of the truth. "Perhaps," he said, "but I plan to be a faithful husband. Our union will be happier if we are compatible lovers."

But Dinah's visage remained frosty. "But *final test* clearly means there were other tests before today." A light went on in her brain. "That was what all our companionable talks were about. You were tallying all my good and bad points, as if I were a prize boar at the county fair, before awarding me a blue ribbon."

Justin shot her a resentful look. "I am no sly schemer. The rebirth of the Sinclair family requires that I choose the mother of the next Earl of Rushmore and my other children carefully. Were I as shallow as you claim, I would reject you, as others of my class would, for your want of dowry or your lack of superior birth." Justin's sense that he was the one being wronged grew. "I did not offer you a slip on the shoulder," he said, testily. "I asked you to marry me. What more do you want?"

Having given Dinah this piece of what he saw as irrefutable logic, Justin expected her to apologize and was shocked when she leaped up and hovered over him.

"Do you love me, Justin?"

He had to lean back on the bench in order to look up into her face. "Love you? What's that to the matter?"

He sounded so incredulous that Dinah went a little berserk. "What kind of man are you that you cannot even pretend to love a woman when you propose to her? I would rather remain a spinster than tie myself to such an unfeeling . . . unfeeling . . ."

When words failed her, Dinah became frustrated and shoved Justin's shoulders with both hands. His arms flailed as he lost his balance, fell backward, and tumbled onto the dirt floor, his long legs still hooked over the seat of the bench.

"What a cow-handed thing to do." He spewed a few choice gutter oaths.

"My sentiments exactly." Dinah threw the words back at him over her shoulder as she escaped from the hut.

Outside in the bright sunshine, she squinted as she looked around the yard. She found a tree stump to use as a mounting block, kicked the mare into a full gallop, and rode off.

* * *

Justin righted himself and thought about going after Dinah, but changed his mind. He was in no mood to deal with a shrew.

He dusted off his backside and sat back down onto the bench. It took only a moment for him to regain his composure.

Damnation! He had made micefeet of his proposal. Apparently, Dinah expected to be loved. Why hadn't he thought of that? He probably should have anticipated having to say the words, even if he did not mean them. But he had never said *I love you* to any woman. He wasn't sure he could; the words would surely stick in his throat.

Justin scratched his head. He had no clue as to how he should proceed now. Dinah was the only woman he wanted for his wife. Somehow a union between them still seemed right, even more so now that he knew she could raise such a hot lust in him. He sighed deeply. But no getting around it; his prospects for winning her hand were seriously diminished after today's fiasco.

Justin got up from the wooden bench with another sigh and made his way to the door, his optimism shaken but not dead. After all, he thought, women were known to change their minds. Dinah was intelligent and would most likely come to her senses once she realized she had thrown away a chance to become a countess.

Chapter 6

Dinah stopped and looked at the sun behind her and knew she was traveling in approximately the right direction. Yet nothing seemed familiar. The fields and the trees and the boulders all looked alike. She fastened the jacket buttons which Justin had undone and whimpered, recalling the sensation of his warm lips on her breasts, but her temper had cooled.

She would not think about him now. She had to get her bearings and find her way home. But how? She thought a moment. She had heard a horse, if given its head, would return to its stable.

Dinah patted the mare's neck. "All right, girl. Let's test the theory. It's up to you." She slackened the reins. The little mare whinnied softly, lifted her head, picked a direction, and trotted off with an air of confidence.

Dinah put her trust in Pansy, while a sick misery engulfed her when the image of Justin sprawled in the dirt in his beautiful red coat leaped into her mind. She groaned. Before today she would have sworn she did not have a violent bone in her body. Now she knew differently.

Dinah shook her head in disbelief. She was a rational creature, not a lunatic who attacked people. Yet she had behaved like a fishwife because a gentleman had failed to pretend he loved her. She sighed in exasperation. What had happened to her calm temperament?

Justin's proposal had been honorable. How could she fault him when he had chosen a wife in a manner which had been bred into his aristocratic bones from the cradle? It would be difficult, but she would have to offer him an apology.

While Pansy covered the distance at a constant amble, Dinah lambasted herself for her stupidity. Justin's kisses had been so intoxicating that she had quite lost all reason. She had wanted Justin to love her. She still wanted him to love her.

The willow trees, their weeping green leaves tinged with yellow, came into view. Four village boys carrying fishing rods called out a greeting to her from beside the rushing brook. She called back, but did not stop. Pansy trotted on toward Sinclair Hall while Dinah hurt.

She could not marry Justin. He wanted a wife who could satisfy his lust, a woman who was prime breeding stock to give him healthy children. He thought he had found these qualities in her. It was enough for him, but not for her. She needed Justin to love her.

Pansy's head came up suddenly and her gait increased to a spirited trot as the barn loomed ahead, with its promise of a clean stall, fresh hay, and cool water.

Sammy set aside the brass carriage lamp he was polishing and rose from his stool when Dinah rode into the yard. He held the mare's head while she slid from the saddle and asked her, "Did you outrun his lordship,

Miss Dinah?" He looked down the bridle path, smiling, as if he expected his employer to come riding in behind her.

Dinah muttered an ambiguous reply, thanked Sammy, and hurried toward home before the good-natured lad could ask any more questions.

Dinah reached her bedroom without being seen. Phoebe was occupied in the kitchen and the children were off playing somewhere. She changed into a prim day dress and went back downstairs, determined to keep her pain to herself.

She was sitting in a comfortable chair beside the fireplace, pretending to read a Richardson novel she had borrowed from Lady Willmer, when Phoebe came into the room.

"Oh, I didn't know you were home, Dinah," Phoebe said, dropping onto the sofa. "Did you enjoy your ride with the earl?"

Dinah put aside her book. She gave Phoebe the same sort of evasive answer she had given Sammy, but was saved from further probing by the sound of the front door opening and the babble of children's voices.

"We're in here," Phoebe called to the youngsters.

Lily ran into the room and climbed up onto the sofa beside Phoebe and leaned into her adopted aunt's shoulder. Phoebe hugged the child to her and kissed her small forehead.

"Sidney was mean to me," Lily complained. Phoebe tut-tutted in mock commiseration.

Trailed by Malcolm and Martha, Sidney marched into the room, and gave his side of the squabble.

Phoebe sorted things out and mended the children's wounded sensibilities.

From the man's chair he had commandeered, Sidney said to Dinah, "Since you went riding with Lord Nabob today, can we go to the hall for our lessons with Mr. O'Shay tomorrow?"

Caught off guard, Dinah felt a sinking sensation. How could she take the children to Justin's estate when she was still too embarrassed to face him? Falling back on a convenient lie which popped into her fertile mind, she said. "I think we have been taking unfair advantage of his lordship's kindness. We must curtail our visits for a time."

"What does *curtail* mean?" Lily asked, frowning, for the word did not sound promising.

"It means we can't go to the hall as much," Sidney illuminated his sister. "When can we go, Dinah? Lord Nabob said we could come every single day. My skills are going to get rusty."

"I doubt it, Sidney," Dinah replied as the children stared at her with expectant eyes. Malcolm was sprawled on the floor; Martha sat in a wing chair.

"Lord Nabob wants us to visit him," Lily said, seconding Sidney. "Dulcie will be *sooo* sad if I don't come to see her. She will have nobody to play with."

Dinah sighed. The hound would not expire from loneliness, but she chose not to quibble with them.

"Lord Rushmore and I have had a serious disagreement," she said, depending on the truth to satisfy the children. "I no longer feel comfortable taking favors from the earl."

Phoebe raised an inquisitive brow, but said nothing.

"It's not fair," Malcolm groused, shattering Dinah's expectations for a quick compliance. "We like Lord Nabob."

"You are always preaching that we should not hold a grudge," Sidney said. "Why don't you resolve your quarrel with his lordship? Why must we suffer?"

The three younger children ganged up on her until Martha intervened. "Be quiet," she said and turned to Dinah. "Can't we go anyway by ourselves? Lord Nabob is a kind man. He would not hold it against us that you and he are at daggers drawn."

Dinah blessed Martha. "You are right, Martha," she said, snatching at the lifeline. "His lordship would not take his discontent with me out on you children. You can go to the hall without me. Mr. O'Shay and Sammy will look after you."

"Oh, no," Phoebe cried in dismay. "Dinah, what are you thinking? We could not foist the children on his lordship's employees without your being there to supervise them. The earl will think we are a pack of encroaching mushrooms who don't know our place."

The children pouted, but did not argue with their Aunt Phoebe. Dinah, though, continued to receive black looks until her resolution wavered.

"All right," she snapped. "Don't make a great dust of it. I am promised to Lady Willmer in the morning, but I shall take you to the hall tomorrow afternoon."

Led by Sidney, the children gave a victorious cheer and moved off to the corner of the room where the built-in shelves held their books and games.

Phoebe stared expectantly at Dinah and waited.

Dinah made a small, ineffectual sound of protest before she pleaded, "I cannot explain, Phoebe. It is personal."

But Phoebe was not to be forestalled. She said, "Your outing with Lord Rushmore was not pleasant."

When Dinah merely shrugged, Phoebe bit her lower lip and kept her voice low so that the children would not hear her. "Lud, Dinah, if he made improper advances, you must not go to the hall. I will make the children understand that we must cut the connection."

Dinah shook her head, flushing slightly. "I am the one who owes Lord Rushmore an apology. But could we please drop the subject? I promise to make it right with him for the children's sake, as well as my own peace of mind."

Phoebe's curiosity was sharpened by Dinah's secrecy, but she respected her friend's privacy. She took up her knitting without another word while Dinah opened Richardson's *Virtue Rewarded* and pretended to read.

But Dinah was reprieved from her promise to take the children to Sinclair Hall when Henry Chasen came by the same afternoon with an invitation for the Connors to join him and his two children the next day at the traveling fair which had set up in a field near Carnbury Village.

"I am driving the wagon, so there will be plenty of room," Henry said to Phoebe. "My cousin Ralph has volunteered to come with me and keep an eye on the children. You need not fear one of them will be kidnapped by the gypsies."

Phoebe laughed at his joke and assured him she knew the children would be safe with him. She offered Henry a cup of tea, but he declined, citing a long list of errands Arlene, his wife, had entrusted to him.

Phoebe had said nothing to Henry about moving, and he wondered about it. A few days before, he had given Justin advice about reviving his agricultural operations. The conversation had shifted to Dick, Hobie, and Masters and the hunting fortnight in January. At that time, Justin had made some oblique reference to negotiations with Mrs. Barrow, but something sidetracked their talk and Henry never heard the rest of it, but he knew Justin's hunting plans were still on.

Although Phoebe was a friend, Henry did not feel comfortable delving into a subject as sensitive as her business dealings with Justin. He might be borrowing trouble if she thought he was pumping her for information.

"I shall pick up the Connors at eleven," he said and left with his curiosity unabated.

The next day when Dinah came home from Lady Willmer's, she saw Justin's horse Jasper tied to the brass hitching post in the drive. Her first chickenhearted impulse was to flee to the garden and wait for him to leave. But she was curious to know what he was up to and reluctant to leave Phoebe unprotected, so she went inside, hung up her bonnet on a hook next to the door, and walked into the main room, where Justin sat beside Phoebe on the sofa.

He rose and waited for her to be seated before he sat down again. One look at Phoebe, and Dinah knew her concern for her friend had not been misplaced.

Justin looked cool and in control, but Phoebe's smile was wan and forced when she said, "Lord Rushmore's agent has found a house he thinks would be suitable for our family."

Moved by the sadness in Phoebe's eyes, Dinah declared, "Phoebe, you have every right to stay until the lease runs out this summer. Why rush things?"

Justin's wide brow puckered. "Frankly, Miss Monroe, I am tired of hearing that refrain." He had been allowing her to dictate the terms. It was time he applied some needed heat and put a little scare in her.

Turning to Phoebe, he said, "Mrs. Barrow, I would not let Miss Monroe's well-meaning but wrongheaded advice cause you to do something foolish."

Stung by his words, Dinah was momentarily speechless.

"I have every confidence," he said, "that a judge would set aside the six months left on the lease if he heard the generous compensations I have offered. I assure you if the matter went to court, Mrs. Barrow, you would lose and would have spent your money for a lawyer needlessly."

Dinah was horrified. A lawyer? Where would they get the money to hire a lawyer? Surely Justin would not really sue them.

"You have no call to frighten Mrs. Barrow," she said, for Phoebe had gone very pale when he mentioned going to court.

It was not what Justin wanted. Mrs. Barrow was not the problem. She would have succumbed to his wishes long ago. Dinah was the one who needed to be persuaded.

"Miss Monroe, neither of us would gain from such a move. We would only enrich some solicitors' pocketbooks," Justin admitted. "But consider what would happen if I did. By the time Mrs. Barrow's petition got on the docket and a date for a trial was set, months would go by. I would be surprised if the case were heard much before the summer. I would take over in June, and Mrs. Barrow would forfeit everything I have offered. Yes, I would lose the use of the lodge for the hunting season, but is it worth giving up all the money involved simply to thwart my desires when the ultimate outcome will not change?"

Justin read the only possible answer in their faces.

After a moment of silence, he said, gently, "You need not make up your mind right now. Think about it. Let me drive Mrs. Barrow to inspect the house tomorrow, Miss Monroe. Perhaps you would like to come with us."

"I have to work tomorrow," Dinah said, all her indignation gone. She had promised to write out Lady Willmer's Christmas correspondence, which had to be posted the next day. "Where is the property of which you speak, my lord?"

Justin named Bresley, a town some ten miles to the west of Carnbury Village. He discussed the house and its environs for another few minutes before he stood up. Dinah got up with him.

"I will bring my carriage around at ten o'clock," he said to Phoebe. "Mr. O'Shay is not a seasoned coachman, but I have not hired a professional driver as yet." His grin was friendly. "However, I do not expect Mr. O'Shay will run us into a ditch."

From politeness, Phoebe smiled at the earl's flat jest. He unnerved her. He was overpowering and seemed to have a will of iron.

Dinah surprised Justin when she announced, "I will see his lordship to his horse," and fell into step beside him.

Outside on the drive, she said, "I would have a word with you, Justin."

"Let it go, Dinah," Justin replied. "Regardless of what Mrs. Barrow decides about the Bresley house, I mean to have the lodge for the hunting season."

"What I have to say is not about the lodge, but about our . . . our encounter at the sheepherder's hut."

Justin's brow lifted, and he looked at her with interest.

Nervously, Dinah's fingers twitched the button at her neckline. "I beg your pardon, my lord, for tumbling you from the bench. I cannot imagine what got into me. I have never laid a hand in anger on anyone before."

Justin chuckled and treated the incident lightly. "Heaven only knows how my consequence would suffer if word got around that I had been bested in a donnybrook by a female who comes up to my chin and possesses half my weight." He gave her his best toe-curling grin. "Next time I shall stay alert and get in the first punch."

"I cannot imagine you lifting your hand against any woman." Dinah had not spent all those days with him without knowing something of his character.

"Ah, romantic illusions," he mocked playfully. "Does that mean you wish to accept my proposal?"

Dinah shook her head. The cocky smile vanished from Justin's lips.

"No?" he said.

"I am sensible of the honor you pay me, my lord, but, no. I cannot marry you." Dinah had called herself all manners of a fool for being unable to settle for a one-sided love affair when she had so much to gain.

Justin sighed. "I suppose it is the love thing. I do care for you, but I fear what you want is some sort of pledge of undying love. I could lie, but I won't." He stood beside her, tall and resolute.

He untied his horse and mounted in one fluid motion. "Should you change your mind, Dinah, you can make your wishes known to me. But two proposals and two rejections are my limit. I shall not ask again."

Dinah found his civil tone difficult to endure. She could not be very important to him if he were unwilling to chance another proposal. To save her pride, she looked down at the ground, for if Justin should gaze full into her eyes, he was bound to see her hurt and how much she loved him.

By the time Dinah raised her head, Justin had dug his heels into Jasper's side and ridden away and left her in an untenable position. He had made it clear he was incapable of loving her. She went through several arguments with her inner voice, but, sadly, she could not imagine a single circumstance where she could bring herself to *make her wishes known to him,* as he had put it.

Chapter 7

When Dinah heard Justin's traveling coach come rattling down the drive, she leaned toward the window beside her chair and peered through the sheer curtains. She laid aside the stocking she was darning for Malcolm and watched Mr. O'Shay pull hard on the reins to bring the carriage horses to a stop.

The coach's door sprang open; Justin jumped down onto the drive and pulled the steps into place. Dinah had told herself she was getting over the earl, but she felt a rush of desire at the sight of him, looking handsome decked out in the conservatively stylish attire befitting a nabob.

Phoebe's black-bonneted head emerged from the coach. She accepted the earl's gloved hand and stepped down onto the graveled drive. Justin bowed briefly over Phoebe's fingers before he leaped back into the passenger compartment, pulling the door closed behind him.

The coach turned around in the circular drive and was gone by the time Phoebe came into the main room and collapsed into a wing chair. Dinah remained sitting by the window, her mending in her lap. "You are going to say the house the earl showed you is horrible," she ventured.

Phoebe shook her head. "I shan't say anything of the sort. It is a fine property, in excellent repair."

She set the cloth reticule she clutched in her hands down on an end table, stripped off her black cotton gloves, and laid them beside the purse.

"You must have seen some drawbacks, or you would not look so Friday-faced."

At Dinah's words, Phoebe released a wail of strictures. "I just don't want to move. The houses in Bresley are close together, the street is trafficky, the garden is small. Where would we grow our vegetables? Where would the children play? It is not country."

"You don't have to take it," Dinah said for the hundredth time. "Stay here until June."

Phoebe sighed wearily. "Suppose the earl changes his mind and takes us to court. Then what? We don't have the money to fight him."

"Fustian," Dinah said, picking up the stocking she had been mending for Malcolm and jamming the needle into the heel. "I know his lordship. You heard him. He doesn't want to sue us. I still think, though, that if we hold firm he may change his mind about letting us stay."

"Oh, Dinah, I am tired of it all," Phoebe moaned, "but if there were only a way."

Dinah and Phoebe went over the same territory which had been the main thrust of endless conversations and discussions since Lord Rushmore had come home from India. But the conclusions remained the same. Phoebe had no desire to be uprooted from the country and give up the home she had come to love, and the earl was determined to entice her into doing his bidding by using his unlimited wealth as leverage.

Dinah finished her darning, rolled Malcolm's stocking together with its pair, and added the black hose to the clean laundry in the basket at her feet.

She looked at Phoebe, mired in gloom, and thought, *Suppose I agree to marry Justin if he promises to let Phoebe live in the lodge?* In truth, she would not be making a real sacrifice. And Justin, on his part, was a realist and in the habit of making business deals. Yet beginning a marriage with a form of blackmail was sheer stupidity.

Dinah sighed. She could never bring herself to implement such a base scheme, even as repayment for Phoebe's giving her a home when she was destitute and had nowhere to go.

"What are you going to do?" she asked.

With more nobility than truth, Phoebe said, "I will accept the earl's generous terms with good grace and consider myself fortunate."

Something in Dinah wanted to battle on, but she remembered Justin's warning and, through a dint of will, she managed to keep from urging Phoebe to reconsider. The money could make a real difference in their lives. But she could not resist asking, "Is that what you truly want to do?"

"No," Phoebe said with a shrug of defeat. "But Lord Rushmore is a man who is adept at getting his way, and I am no match for him." Yet in keeping with her character, she added charitably, "But we must give the man his due. The property is his to do with as he wishes. Often men with Lord Rushmore's resources are miserly and disinclined to part with their money. I cannot accuse the earl of cheeseparing. Financially, he is leaving us better off than we have ever been."

Dinah could not dispute Phoebe's frank appraisal of

Justin, although she could not help thinking that having money made it a lot easier for him to be altruistic.

But all of the fight went out of her. "You are turning the lodge back to him," she said.

Although Phoebe was heartbroken, she held her head high in final capitulation. "Yes. It is the most sensible, the most intelligent, thing to do."

Dinah sat on a wooden bench in the shade of an oak tree where she and Justin had spent many days in companionable conversations. The bench faced the arena, where Mr. O'Shay was teaching the three older Connor children to ride. Nearby, Lily tumbled in the grass with Dulcie.

Dinah heard footsteps coming through the copse and knew without looking it was Justin.

"I am glad you came today, Dinah," he said, looking pleased to see her. "I hoped we could remain friends despite what has passed between us."

Justin put his booted foot on the seat of the bench and leaned his arms on his knee. He looked dashing in a brown jacket and suede breeches.

Dinah banked down the love which shot through her. She shaded her eyes against the sun and looked up at him. "I could not bring the children if we were not civil to one another," she said dismissively.

His smile slipped away. He mocked, "Civil for the children's sake. So sensible. So vapid."

Dinah scolded herself for sounding cold, but, really, what could she have said that was nearer the truth?

Justin removed his foot from the bench and stood looking down at her. "I want us to be friends."

Dinah shrugged. "We are," she said.

Justin was not convinced by the puny reply. His features became an impersonal mask. "Mrs. Barrow seemed to like the Bresley house," he said.

Dinah blinked at the abrupt change of subject. "Not really," she replied unwisely, but with incurable honesty.

His composure already disturbed by what he saw as a rebuff of his offer of friendship, Justin became truly annoyed, for it was definitely not what he wanted to hear. "What is wrong now?"

"Children need space to play. They will lose the freedom to enjoy the outdoors they have here in the country."

Justin pushed out his chin defiantly. "Every time I make an accommodation with Mrs. Barrow, you squelch it. I have deep pockets, Dinah. Let's end this once and for all. Since you seem to be in charge, not the widow, give me a figure in hard cash that will satisfy you."

Dinah sucked in her breath. Her brown eyes became as steely as his blue ones. "You think every impediment can be removed with money, Justin. What you don't comprehend is that your lavish monetary offers do not buy happiness. Happiness, to Phoebe, is the lodge. I do not think you realize what that house means to her."

Justin glowered down at her. "Mrs. Barrow will learn to like the Bresley house," he said stubbornly, then turned on his heel, walked over to the ring, and leaned on the fence to watch Sidney putting a horse called Mercury through its paces under Mr. O'Shay's watchful eyes.

Dinah stared at Justin's broad back and fumed. He had a lot of gall accusing her of attempting to fleece him by manipulating Phoebe. He had turned his back on her once before during a disagreement, and she had caved in, but not this time. She would not let the insult stand.

She walked over to Justin and pulled his shoulder

around to make him face her. "How dare you say my interest in helping Phoebe is mercenary? That's a lie."

She was surprised when she saw him flinch. She looked into his bright blue eyes and realized his anger was not with her, but with himself.

"I know money does not tempt you, Dinah," he said, "or else we would already be betrothed."

She found his directness more sincere than some gentlemanly obligatory apology.

He gave her a rueful smile. "Let's stop bickering and be friends."

"We are," she said again, but this time her voice was animated.

Suddenly, Justin wanted to take her in his arms and kiss her, but he saw nothing in her demeanor to encourage such unwarranted intimacy. In fact, she seemed to be mulling over something unpleasant. He decided he would be better served by getting away from her. Since that day in Silas's hut when she had gone soft and pliant in his arms, he had been having erotic dreams about her. Last night he had actually fantasized about what it might be like spending the rest of his life making love to her.

He would saddle Jasper and leave before he did something foolish like asking her to take tea with him at the hall in order to get her alone so he could act on his feelings. But he needed some diversion during his ride to stop him from thinking of how her warm and eager lips had moved under his.

In a burst of inspiration, Justin said, "Sidney is ready to try his wings. If you don't object, I will take him for a gallop as far as the brook."

"Now?"

"Yes, you don't have to wait around. I will bring him to Mrs. Barrow's when we return," he said.

"That will be fine, Justin," Dinah said crisply, "but before you go, we must put an end to the matter of Phoebe and the lodge."

Justin moaned. Why couldn't she drop the subject? He was not going to change his mind.

But Dinah ignored the inarticulate sound. "Justin, I was not forthcoming with you," she said. "Phoebe has decided to accept your terms and rent the house in Bresley. It was wrong of me to imply she was still wavering."

Justin looked at her in surprise. He should have felt a sense of triumph, but he did not.

He nodded and walked off to have a word with Mr. O'Shay before going into the stables and emerging shortly, leading Jasper. He mounted the horse.

When Sidney rode from the confines of the ring to join Justin, he was smiling from ear to ear. On Mercury, he followed the earl's horse down the bridle path.

Malcolm groused about being left behind, but Mr. O'Shay tousled the boy's red hair affectionately. "You will have your chance, lad," he promised, "when you have had a bit more practice."

Holding Lily's hand, Dinah walked home slowly. Martha and Malcolm raced ahead, each child wanting to be the first to tell their Aunt Phoebe that Sidney had gone riding with Lord Nabob.

Dinah was aware her days here on the earl's estate were numbered. Once she and Phoebe moved to the house in Bresley, she would be ten miles away, too far to walk to Sinclair Hall.

Lily chattered away nonstop. Every so often Dinah would smile down at her, knowing Lily took the smiles as a sign Dinah was listening.

Dinah wondered how things would change once she moved. She supposed she would remain Justin's friend—

at least until he married and their friendship died a natural death. But when she imagined Justin married to someone else, something inside her recoiled. No! No! She would not think of that. It hurt too much.

Lily looked up at Dinah and gave her a puzzled look. "Why did you squish my hand so hard, Dinah?"

But Dinah could not speak, for all of a sudden her throat had thickened from the profound sadness in her heart.

Chapter 8

Sidney could not stop smiling as he rode beside Justin over the stark fields, which were more brown than green. He sat erect in the saddle, as he had been taught.

"This is top of the trees, Lord Nabob," he said, his freckled face beaming. "You are a great gun for suggesting it."

Justin said, more forcefully than he intended, "Don't get carried away in your enthusiasm, lad. You need to remain alert when you are riding."

Sidney nodded, all seriousness. "Yes, I know. Mr. O'Shay warned me to be on the lookout for hidden rabbit holes and birds flying up from the fields and unseen animals jumping from the bushes that could spook Mercury. I promise I shall keep my wits about me and a tight rein on him."

"See that you do," Justin said, but he was not really worried. Mercury was a docile creature, unlike his Roman god namesake. But riding accidents were common with beginning riders.

Yet the earl winced when the boy seemed to have taken his admonition to heart. Sidney scowled fiercely and peered intently at the ground and the dense underbrush which skirted the bridle path.

If he exhorted the lad to relax after warning him to keep alert, he would confuse Sidney and seem overly controlling. Justin wanted the boy to enjoy his first long ride rather than view it as a chore. His criticism was the sort adults made carelessly and which caused novice riders to begin to doubt themselves.

Making conversation, Justin kept his tone deliberately offhand. "Have you had schooling, Sidney?"

"Oh, yes, Lord Nabob," the boy said, proudly. He raised his head, as Justin hoped he would, and glanced over at him. Bits of red hair stuck out from around the tweed cap he wore. "My pa insisted we learn to read and write, even Martha. Lily was only a babe when he died. But Dinah's teaching her to read now."

"Was your father a stern taskmaster?" Justin asked, keeping the conversation going to divert the lad from his unnatural concentration on his surroundings.

Sidney guffawed. "Believe it, my lord. He was a sergeant in the King's army, but he was what Dinah calls a benevolent dictator. Pa did not hold with a person just making his mark and not understanding what he was signing. The world is populated with unscrupulous persons ready to take advantage of the uneducated, you know."

Justin's ploy had worked. The boy relaxed as the earl chatted with him. He was no longer staring nervously at the ground.

Justin looked out on the wintry landscape with its leafless trees. The air was pleasantly cool, but not icy as it would have been in some parts of England in December. He was impressed with Sidney's intelligence. The boy was bright and talked sense.

They rode on discussing this and that when Sidney said, "I know your story from the talk in the village, Lord Nabob. But I always wondered how you got the fare to board a ship to India if you were left destitute."

"I found a fair amount of cash which my father had hidden in a safe behind a picture in his study, along with a few worthless jewels that had belonged to my late mother. I removed enough money for my passage," Justin said.

Sidney cocked his head. "Why did you not take all of the money?"

Justin smiled a little. "I suspected once the premises were searched by the authorities, the hiding place would be discovered. Lord Dekker might have sent one of his henchmen after me before I left England if the safe was empty. But the presence of the remaining money and the jewels would lead him to believe I knew nothing about my father's secret cache."

Sidney gave Justin a canny grin. "You are a downy one, Lord Nabob," he said admiringly.

Justin's lips twitched at the ingenuous compliment. He told Sidney the rest of what happened before he began his odyssey to India. To foil the sheriff's men, who searched his person and his single valise before Justin was allowed to leave Sinclair Hall for good, Henry Chasen had kept the money for him. He told the wide-eyed boy, "Mr. Chasen met me the night I left for the coast to board the ship for the Far East and turned the money back to me and wished me Godspeed."

They reached the brook where Justin and Dinah had stopped near the willow tree a few days before. Sidney sat on the same log as had Dinah and watched the horses drinking from the stream.

Justin dropped down beside the boy and stretched his long legs in front of him. His conscience had suffered whenever he remembered the dalliance he had so carelessly planned to foist on Dinah that day. Countless times he had reproached himself for his reprehensible conduct at the hut. It was not one of his more noble moments.

"Dinah brings us here in the summertime for picnics and fishing," Sidney said, bringing Justin back to the present. "I love the country. You know, sir, Carnbury Village is the best place I have ever lived. And the lodge is the very best house by far. I never had a room all to myself before. Wherever we followed my father and the army, I shared a bed with Malcolm. The worst was in Brussels. Martha and Lily slept with us in the same room. It was horrible during the battle. Ma died, and then we heard that Pa and Captain Barrow had been killed."

Justin found himself interested. "Is that when Mrs. Barrow took over your care?"

Sidney needed no prodding. He was eager to tell his story. "Yes. Aunt Phoebe was as brave as any soldier. She marshalled help from the men under Captain Barrow's command to see to the burials. When she brought us back to England, she contacted our relatives, but no one would take us. Her brother, who lives nearby, was willing to give her a home, but only if she put us in an orphanage. She wasn't our real aunt or any kin to us at all, but she was determinded to keep us together. Wasn't that nice?"

Justin nodded. He got up from the log, whistled the horses over to him, and said brusquely, "I'd best get you back to the lodge. Mrs. Barrow will be wondering what's become of us."

Wasn't that nice? Sidney had asked him. *Damn,* Justin thought as he plodded along on Jasper. *Nice? The woman was a saint.* But a man had a right to his own property. And it wasn't as though he had cheated Mrs. Barrow. He had volunteered to return her rent and had found her a superior replacement house, all at his expense.

By the time the lodge came into view and he saw Dinah and the three Connor children waiting for Sidney on the steps, he was sternly lecturing himself about letting sentiment interfere with business.

Sidney slid from Mercury's back and secured the reins to a hitching post. He was immediately surrounded by his brother and sisters and Dinah. Phoebe came from the house to join them, wiping her hands on her calico apron. Everyone was talking at once and bombarding Sidney with questions.

In all the babble, Justin heard Phoebe say, "My! My! Sidney, I am that proud of you." The boy beamed. Justin dismounted. He stood apart from the merriment, his eyes on Dinah.

A faint smile brought on by the sweet sound of her laughter peeped through his solemn expression. She was a beautiful, loving, and caring person. He had come to love her, but, alas, she would never believe him now. He despaired he would ever again hold her in his arms and feel her clinging to him as if she never wanted to let him go, as she had in Silas's hut.

Dinah saw the doleful expression in Justin's eyes and wondered what he was thinking to cause him to look mournful when everyone else was in high spirits.

Lily ran to him and tugged on his coattails, bringing a smile to his face.

"Lord Nabob, Lord Nabob," she cried, looking up at him, her blue eyes sparkling, "we are having a Christmas party and are baking cookies."

"Cookies?" Justin raised an inquiring brow at Dinah.

"Cookies are the American name for sweet biscuits," Dinah said.

Justin rolled his eyes. "Oh, yes, the American Christmas—or is it Dutch?"

"Both, my lord. The Dutch settled in America," Martha said in her grown-up voice. "Oh, Dinah, let's invite Lord Nabob to the Christmas party," she added.

"What a splendid notion, Martha." Sidney brushed past his sister to stand at Justin's side. He looked up at the earl. "You must come, Lord Nabob. It will be on Christmas Eve."

Lily began to dance up and down on one foot, then the other. "Please, please come."

Not to be outdone, Malcolm added an entreaty to Dinah. "Say Lord Nabob can come to bake the cookies. Tell him."

"I imagine Lord Rushmore is already spoken for on Christmas Eve," Dinah said, although she, too, wanted him to accept the children's invitation.

"As a matter of fact, ma'am, I am free that evening and would be delighted to join all of you." On his desk at Sinclair Hall were a few invitations to gatherings in London. He had yet to send his regrets, but he would now. "Of course, I would not want to intrude," he said, looking at Mrs. Barrow. She might not want him as a guest during her last days in the lodge.

But as always, Phoebe was courteous. "You would not be intruding, my lord. You would be most welcome."

"Thank you," he said, picking up her hand and kissing her fingertips, causing her to blush. The children surrounded him, all of them talking at the same time.

Justin gazed into Dinah's soft brown eyes. She was the only woman he wanted to bear him the sons he needed to insure his family's lineage. Without Dinah, any marriage he would enter into would be joyless and empty.

Dinah could not take her eyes from him as the children followed him to his horse and crowded around him. From the saddle, he looked over their heads and captured her eyes again.

A special sort of smile touched his lips. If Dinah had not known better, she might have suspected Justin had fallen in love with her. But of course she knew better.

Yet as he rode away, leading the horse which Sidney had borrowed, she found their friendship comforting. Perhaps in time . . . she let the thought trail off unfinished.

Chapter 9

Early in the evening on Christmas Eve, Justin rapped on the door of the lodge, wearing a many-caped coat, for the air was unusually crisp and wintery. Dinah let him in, took his outer garment, and hooked it up on a wall peg while he placed his beaver hat and leather gloves on a hall table. She looked so pleased to see him that Justin's heart went warm.

The lodge had a pleasant woodsy smell from the evergreen boughs with which Dinah had decorated the hall. Justin followed her as she led him toward the back of the house, her heather gray skirts swirling around her trim ankles.

In the kitchen, he was met with a chorus of exuberant greetings from the children, which he returned with hearty responses of his own. He bowed elegantly to Phoebe, which made her feel as if she were the grandest lady in society.

"Your nose is red, Lord Nabob," Lily said, giggling.

"The winter air is quite nippy this evening," Justin

admitted, smiling down at the child in her blue dress and white pinafore. "We may have snow by morning." The unexpected declaration brought a flood of stunned responses.

"Snow for Christmas?" Lily said. "Dinah told us it would take a miracle for it to snow here."

"Then we may be in for a miracle, poppet," Justin said, winking at her.

Malcolm frowned. "But, Dinah, when we were looking at the scenes of Christmas in a picture book, you said we are too far south for snow."

"And I stand by my contention," she said with a mischievous toss of her blond topknot. "Lord Rushmore is funning."

Justin enjoyed the byplay. "It felt to me like snow was in the air as I walked across the fields from the hall. I even wore my winter coat for the first time tonight."

"It may be cold," Dinah said, her eyes dancing, "but when have you ever seen snow on Christmas in our part of England, my lord?"

"I distinctly remember snow falling when I was nine or ten," Justin said to stir the pot of controversy and keep up the banter with Dinah, which he found amusing.

The decibel level of rendered opinions rose significantly as each person, large and small, weighed in on the possibilities or probabilities or likelihoods that Christmas morning would see snow.

Phoebe put an end to the fascinating subject when it looked like the discussion was going to go on forever. "I think it is time we concentrated on mixing the batter for the cookies."

The ingredients were already spread over the large table, which was used daily for preparing meals.

"Stalemate," Justin said in an aside to Dinah before he removed his cobalt blue dress coat and draped it over a wooden chair in the corner, exposing the red silk lining, then rolled up the sleeves of his fine white cambric shirt.

Phoebe assigned everyone a task. Soon Martha and Malcolm were up to their elbows in flour, dusting their play clothes liberally as they sifted the unrefined flour over the mixing bowl. Sidney had a smaller stoneware bowl tucked between his knees and was grunting as he creamed the butter and sugar with a wooden spoon. Justin was given a nutcracker and a bowl of walnuts. Lily sat on a high stool and removed the meats from the cracked nuts that Justin handed her, while Dinah chopped the nut meats into small pieces with a sharp knife on a wooden cutting board.

Phoebe directed the operations and assisted when smaller hands needed help. The room was a cozy warm cocoon on this cold night. The stove had been fired up and the oven was heating nicely.

Justin found he was absurdly content cracking walnuts, replying to bits of childish chatter, and exchanging warm, private glances with Dinah that made his heart beat a little faster. With each passing second, he grew more and more satisfied to be a part of this simple family activity.

The spotless kitchen was well organized. Mrs. Barrow could efficently put her hands on whatever was needed. She looked so right here in her large brown apron, patiently putting up with the neophyte cooks, her ever present kitchen rag speedily cleaning up spills with good grace and a smiling face.

These good children, Dinah, and the widow made Justin feel as if he too belonged to this close-knit blended family. He became convinced children were not only necessary for continuing his aristocratic lineage, but appealing in their own right.

In a single moment of clarity, he understood what Dinah had been trying to make him see when she said it was not about money. Phoebe Barrow had found the haven she had been seeking all of her rootless military life for herself and these orphaned children. One did not put a price on a lady's personal paradise. This was her home, where it pleased her to cook and sweep and scrub and raise her adopted children with unstinting love.

Phoebe looked up from the cookie dough, which she had been mixing in an enormous stoneware bowl. Lord Rushmore gazed at her, a slow smile curling his handsome lips. He seemed almost boyish, unlike the lofty lord she had dealt with in the past. The house he had found for her was large and airy. Some people might even see it as a definite improvement over the lodge.

As painful as it was to give up her utopia, it was time she was sensible. For once, she had acted with her mind rather than with her heart. She gave Lord Rushmore a rather wistful smile.

Second thoughts about the lodge had been popping up in Justin's mind more and more since his ride with Sidney. He felt his resolution becoming further undermined as he met the sweet sadness in Phoebe's eyes. Her selfless decency made his own desires seem shallow. Suddenly, he knew exactly what he was going to do and began to hum happily.

Dinah used two spoons, one to scoop and one to push the small mounds of dough onto the tin baking sheets. Phoebe took up the pair of pans and slipped them into the hot oven. "We need to keep a close watch on the biscuits," she said.

"Cookies, not biscuits, Aunt Phoebe," Martha said. "Americans call biscuits cookies."

Phoebe smiled at the child. "Pardon me, Martha. I forgot. We must keep a close watch on the *cookies* so that they do not burn." Justin thought that, just like Dinah, the widow was good with children. She had a patient, gentle way with them.

"How long will it take for the cookies to bake?" Martha asked.

"About ten minutes," Phoebe said, looking at a clock on a shelf above the sink. "But the oven temperature can vary. It is best to check the progress of the baking after five minutes."

Soon a fragrant aroma permeated the kitchen. "I can smell the cookies," Sidney said, sniffing the air.

"Me too, me too," came from Lily and Malcolm.

Phoebe checked the cookies after five minutes, but shook her head to indicate the baked goods were not yet ready.

When Phoebe opened the oven door a second time, the children crowded around her and craned their necks to see inside.

"Perfect," the widow declared and removed the baking tins one at a time with an old pot holder whose original yellow color was singed brown from frequent use.

Dinah brought a pitcher of eggnog, which she had mixed earlier, from the pantry. Phoebe removed seven cups from the kitchen shelf and lined them up on a tray for Dinah to fill.

With a spatula, the widow removed the cookies, called Jumbles, piecemeal to a large platter which Justin remembered as having been used to serve venison in his father's day.

Justin put on the coat he had discarded earlier and helped move the Christmas Eve repast to the heavy oak table in the dining area of the main room. A matching sideboard that would not have looked out of place in a king's castle stood against one wall.

The furniture in the main room was familiar to Justin. Years ago he and his schoolmates had sprawled on the oversized chairs and sofas while they sang bawdy songs and tittered like girls over off-color jokes, as young boys were wont to do.

Most of the upholstered pieces were about thirty years old, while the wooden dining table, the sideboard, and the armoires in the bedrooms above had been purchased by his grandfather when he had built the lodge some ninety years before.

"You have done an admirable job, Mrs. Barrow, in polishing the furniture and keeping the family possessions in excellent repair," Justin said, complimenting her housekeeping.

"The furnishings are of the best quality," Phoebe said, basking in the praise. "I know everything from the furniture on the lower floors to the magnificently carved bedsteads in the bedrooms were selected with masculine tastes in mind. However, I have found all of it very beautiful and a pleasure to care for."

Justin remained standing until the women and the children were seated around the table before he took the unoccupied chair beside Dinah. His arm nearest to her brushed against her shoulder, and Dinah felt a tingle spread through her at the inadvertent touch. His appearance here tonight filled her with happiness. Her feelings for him had become so strong she knew if he relented and asked for her hand again she would be hard put to retreat a third time.

The children attacked the Jumbles, warm from the oven, with gusto.

"Oh, what a treat!" Lily cried. Phoebe smiled, for the household budget rarely allowed for sweets of any sort, which made the cookies extra special. She was glad Dinah had insisted on this Christmas celebration, for the Connor children had had very little joy in their short lives. For a moment, she felt melancholy knowing this would be the last Christmas they would celebrate in this house, but she forced the sad emotion aside.

Justin thought he would never eat a sweet biscuit again without thinking of this remarkable evening. He had dined with rajahs and royalty, but never had he enjoyed himself more.

Laughter filled the dining room, along with easy chatter, as the youngsters drank their eggnog and stuffed themselves with the fresh-baked cookies. The three adults ate more judiciously, intentionally leaving the major portion of the goodies for the children.

Without prompting, Sidney began to sing the familiar *God Rest Ye Merry Gentlemen* in a clear boy soprano. Dinah joined in, and Justin followed. Phoebe listened as the earl's fine baritone joined with her friend's sweet contralto. Then everyone sang. The lodge did not have a pianoforte, so the amateur chorus sang a cappella. When their repertoire of carols was exhausted, Dinah retold the Dutch tale of Saint Nicholas. The children never tired of hearing how the old gentleman drove a wagon through the sky above the treetops.

"He dropped oranges and sugarplums and gifts down the chimney pots," she said, pausing for dramatic effect, "and by magic, the presents landed unerringly in the various stockings hung by the fire."

"Like the stockings you made for us, Dinah," Lily said, her child's eyes big. The little girl pointed to the red flannel oversized stockings pinned to the mantel of the fieldstone fireplace on the other end of the huge room.

Phoebe glanced at the longcase clock in the corner and proclaimed it was well past the children's bedtime. After the usual moans and groans, the redheaded brothers and sisters marched toward the stairs, shouting, "Good night, Lord Nabob."

He answered, "Sleep well, children."

Phoebe and Dinah excused themselves and left to tuck the children into bed.

When the room had cleared, Justin went to the fireplace. He reached into his coat pocket and removed four gold coins. Carefully, he dropped a sovereign into the toe of each stocking.

He walked back to the table and collected the cups and soiled napkins and piled them onto the tray he had used to bring the eggnog from the kitchen. He had never tasted the rich drink before. He hadn't liked it much. Personally, he thought, he would have preferred a hot spicy wassail.

The two women came back into the room. "Oh, Lord Rushmore," Phoebe protested, a flush on her round cheeks. "Dinah and I shall do that." She had never seen a man who was not a servant clear a table before. But then she would never have believed a lord would roll up his sleeves and help bake cookies and rub along as if he were one of them.

Afraid he was embarrassing Phoebe, Justin put down the cup in his hand.

"I can truthfully say, Mrs. Barrow, that I have not enjoyed a Christmas celebration as much since I was a strapling."

Phoebe beamed at the sincerity in his deep voice.

Dinah walked Justin to the front door and helped him into his coat. She handed him his hat and gloves, opened the door, and stepped onto the porch. Looking up into the sky, she wrapped her arms around herself against the chill. "No stars visible tonight," she said.

"Snow clouds," Justin claimed. He leaned over and kissed her on the cheek. "Thank you for a lovely evening."

Their eyes met, and for an instant Dinah thought he looked changed. Before she could make anything of this fanciful impression, Justin leaped down the stairs and walked briskly off into the night.

"You know, Dinah, I do love you," came in a whisper from somewhere in the darkness, so soft Dinah questioned her ears. Was it imagination or real?

She touched the spot on her skin where his warm lips had rested. "I love you, too, Justin Sinclair," she whispered back, even though she knew he was long gone and could not hear her.

Chapter 10

Mid-morning on Christmas Day, Justin stood in front of the lodge, where light snow flew around him, melting as soon as the white flakes hit the ground. The children spilled from the house in their warm coats, shouting and laughing and sticking out their tongues to catch the snowflakes.

"You knew it would snow, Lord Nabob," Malcolm cried. "How did you know?"

Justin looked down into Malcolm's upraised freckled face. "A fortunate guess. I can't really take any credit, lad," he said honestly. "We are simply experiencing a bit of Christmas magic."

The front door opened and Dinah stepped onto the porch. She felt sheer joy at the sight of the earl.

"Come inside, children," she called. "Breakfast is ready. You are invited, too, Lord Nabob." She laughed as she used the same form of address as the children always did. Her laugh sounded like the peal of Christmas bells to Justin. He looked into her beautiful brown eyes across the snowy air and knew just how much he loved her. It was one of the two reasons he was a self-invited guest this morning. The other would make her happy, too, he knew.

Justin took the chair in which he had sat the previous night at the dining table. Dinah gave a Christmas blessing before everyone tucked into their porridge. Justin asked for only coffee, since he had eaten earlier. Phoebe talked him into a currant bun—not their usual fare, but a special holiday treat. She noticed Justin and Dinah could not take their eyes from each other. Phoebe said a silent prayer that Lord Rushmore would look past Dinah's parentage and see all the sterling qualities that would make her as fine a countess as any highborn lady in polite society.

The fire, which had been built up into a respectable blaze against the abnormally cold morning, had burned down. After the meal, Justin offered to add more logs to it.

"Before you do, my lord," Phoebe said, "given your superior height, would you do the honors and remove the stockings from the mantelpiece before the children expire from anticipation?"

Justin took down the first stocking and handed it to Lily, who hugged it to her small chest and waited for her brothers and sister to receive their bounty.

Sidney sat down on the thick hearth rug. He removed the orange and spilled the candies, which were wrapped in colored paper, between his spread legs. His eyes grew large when he spied the shiny coin among the sweets. He stared at the sovereign in disbelief. Picking it up, he examined the money closely.

The other three youngsters by now had found the unexpected treasure. "Is this toy money?" Lily asked.

Dinah bent down and took the coin from the little girl's extended palm. She knew immediately the source of the largess.

"Oh, my," she gasped and stared at Justin, who had busied himself replenishing the logs in the fireplace.

"It's real money, Lily," Dinah said. Phoebe's face softened. Never before had the children been given money of their own.

Justin turned from his chore and met Sidney's eyes. The boy sat less than a foot from him, the coin on his palm.

"Saint Nicholas," Justin warned and Sidney nodded. Martha noted the secret exchange, which confirmed her own suspicions.

Lily gazed up at the high-beamed ceiling and said in a whisper, "Saint Nicholas must have driven his wagon over the rooftop during the night."

Malcolm, too, stared at the ceiling as if trying to peer through it into the December sky.

Phoebe gathered her brood to her. "The gold coins are yours to keep, my dears, but it is a great deal of money. You must spend it wisely." The children nodded solemnly.

Thriftiness was not an alien concept to them, even though they had never before had money to spend on themselves. Lily put the pretty coin in the pocket of her dress, but she was to take it out often during the morning and look at it in wonder.

Justin removed a small book from his own pocket, walked over to where Dinah sat on the sofa beside Phoebe, and handed it to her. "Happy Christmas, Dinah," he said.

She smiled as she accepted the tome. "Shakespeare's sonnets," she said. The book was beautifully bound in leather; the tooled cover had the title and author

stamped in gold. As she riffled the pages, she saw the
poems were lavishly illustrated. It was much grander
than any of the dog-eared books her father had left her.
"Thank you, my lord. I shall treasure it."

Phoebe leaned over and ran a hand over the gold-
leafed scrolls on the cover. "What lovely workmanship,"
she said. She looked up at Justin. "The coins! My lord, I
must thank you on behalf of the children for your generosity." Her voice was too low for anyone but Justin
and Dinah to hear.

Justin reached inside his coat pocket and removed
an official-looking brown envelope tied with a string.
"For you, Mrs. Barrow," he said.

"For me?" Phoebe repeated, as she accepted the
package. She undid the tie, removed the contents, and
read the enclosed pages. Her lips parted in surprise.
Suddenly, she began to sob and laugh at the same time.

Dinah turned to her friend in alarm. "What is wrong,
Phoebe?"

Phoebe waved her hand in the air, but was too
choked up to speak. Dinah gave Justin a curious look
and picked up the letter from Phoebe's lap. She uttered
an enraptured cry. Justin had signed over the lodge to
Phoebe to live in rent free for the rest of her life.

Curious, the children had left the seductive contents
of their stockings to see what had caused their aunt to
weep. But they saw she was not really sad, for she was
smiling through her tears. Finding her voice at last,
Phoebe showed the children the paper and explained
its significance.

Justin had moved to the window in the farthest corner of the room. The snow had stopped. Doing the
right thing had given him more pleasure than he would
ever have imagined.

In the pane of glass, he saw Dinah's reflection as she

came up behind him. She locked her arms around his waist and pressed her cheek against his broad back.

"If you still want me, Justin," she said, swallowing her pride, "I will marry you."

He unclasped her hands and turned from the window to face her. "I do love you," he said.

"I know," she replied. "What about your plans for the hunting parties?"

He gave her a slow, lazy smile and shrugged. "Well, you know how royalty is. Prinny shall take the rescinding of his invitation as a personal affront. He is known to hold a grudge for years. You can forget about ever being received at court, my dear."

Dinah laughed. She was so elated that anything would have made her laugh, but the idea of her, a lowly clergyman's daughter, being invited to hobnob with royalty struck her as ludicrous.

But Dinah thought of Justin's other valued friends. "Your longtime chums—will they hold it against you?"

"Lud, no. Hobie, Dick, and Masters are commonsensical fellows, and Henry is a special friend to you and Phoebe. Neither they nor my acquaintances from India will ring a peal over me when they hear my reasons."

"Only the Prince?"

Justin chuckled. "No, my sweet, not even the Prince. He will want an invitation to the wedding. It would look bad for him if an earl snubbed him. Besides, George has an eye for lovely females. You are so beautiful, my love, that he will take one look at you and forgive me anything." Whereupon, Justin pulled Dinah into his arms and kissed her soundly.

JUMBLES

Jumbles is a cookie name which goes back to colonial times in America. The housewife of that day jumbled together whatever ingredients she had available to make cookies. The recipe for Chocolate Jumbles is a modern day jumbling of popular twenty-first century fixings. Chocolate chips were not available until the 1940s.

But even without the chocolate chips, Dinah would not have been able to bake Chocolate Jumbles at the time of the story, since the process for making cocoa was not developed until 1828 in Holland by C. J. van Houten. However, she and Justin would have had a young family ten years later. I like to think the Sinclairs added this new delicious twist to their Jumbles on Christmas Eve of that year.

Merry Christmas to all Regency fans everywhere.

Alice Holden

CHOCOLATE JUMBLES

½ c. margarine or butter, softened
¾ c. sugar
1 tsp. vanilla
1 egg
1-¼ c. of flour
2 T. cocoa
½ tsp. baking soda
½ c. chocolate chips
½ c. walnuts

Cream margarine and sugar. Add vanilla and egg and mix well. Stir in flour, cocoa, and baking powder. Mix in chocolate chips and walnuts. Using two teaspoons, drop dough onto ungreased baking sheet. Bake at 375 degrees (F) in a preheated oven for 10 to 12 minutes. Makes approximately two dozen cookies.

THE ELUSIVE BRIDE

Debbie Raleigh

Chapter 1

Ian Conner Forrest, Earl of Barclay, regarded the woman hovering in the doorway of his study with a hint of amusement.

Amanda Worthington was certainly not what he had envisioned for his countess. She was not small and elegantly feminine with a natural charm. She was not even, strictly speaking, pretty.

Instead she was long limbed, with an untidy tumble of honey curls and deep green eyes. And as for charming . . . gads, she was blunt to the point of rudeness and far too fond of managing those about her. She did not even possess a sense of fashion, Ian wryly acknowledged, preferring threadbare gowns in gray or brown that she had outgrown years before.

Still, something about her had captivated his interest from the day he had first bought this estate in Surrey.

Perhaps it was her proud grace, which reminded him of a well-bred race horse, or the shrewd intelligence that shimmered in her eyes, or the undeniable courage she had revealed in keeping her father's household from complete ruin.

Whatever the reason, Ian could not deny she had begun to intrude upon his mind with increasing frequency. He could see her attired in beautiful satin gowns that would cling to her lovely curves. She would be standing proudly at his side—or, better yet, lying upon his bed with her magnificent curls spread upon the pillows.

That last vision had kept him awake more nights than he cared to admit, and no doubt had prompted the astonishing notion to make her his wife.

Over the past few weeks, the notion had grown to a certainty. He wanted Amanda Worthington as his countess. Unfortunately, he had been equally certain she would never accept his offer.

Unlike most maidens, she did not anxiously vie to capture his attention. She did not care that he was an earl or that he was considered a most eligible *parti*. In truth, he suspected she did her best to avoid his presence whenever possible.

Which, he was honest enough to admit, only piqued his interest even more.

He had resigned himself to a long, trying courtship with the perverse minx. Amanda was too stubborn and set in her ways to be easily lured into marriage. And then fate, in the form of her scapegrace father, dropped her directly into his lap.

Leaning back in his chair, Ian tapped a slender finger upon the top of the Sheridan desk as he waited for his fiancée to gather her courage to confront him.

Her nervous gaze briefly skimmed his nonchalant form. He knew precisely what she would see. Dark glossy hair that was carefully brushed, lean features with a hint of ruthless determination, and a hard male body currently attired in a dark blue coat and buff breeches. He appeared very much a self-assured earl, with no traces of the years he had spent working side by side with his tenants to save his debt-ridden estate.

His silver eyes narrowed in anticipation as she at last squared her shoulders and stepped into the room. He realized he would have to take great care during this first confrontation.

She was bound to be angry, wary, and determined to save herself from their inevitable marriage. He would have to take a firm hand, he acknowledged ruefully. Amanda Worthington was a woman far too accustomed to having her own way.

Moving with that peculiar grace, she halted in the center of the room. She appeared gloriously composed, despite the horrid gray gown and honey curls that had already strayed from her tidy bun. But Ian did not miss the manner in which her hands were clenched into tight fists at her sides.

"Good afternoon, my lord. I hope I do not intrude?"

"Not at all, Miss Worthington. This is indeed a delightful surprise." Ian rose to his feet and waved an elegant hand toward the chair opposite the desk. "Will you have a seat?"

She paused before stiffly perching on the edge of the chair. "Thank you."

Ian's amusement deepened as he resumed his own seat and stretched out his legs to cross them at the ankle. He was curious to discover how she would launch her battle plan.

"I presume Mrs. Warren will soon be along with tea," he murmured, his hooded gaze studying the pure lines of her handsome countenance—a wide brow, delicate cheekbones, a firm nose, and sensuously carved lips. Yes, he silently acknowledged, with a bit of polish she would make a lovely countess. "I must admit I did not expect you to take it upon yourself to visit Meadowfield. I fully intended to call upon you this evening. I hope your father recalled to warn you that he invited me to dinner?"

"Yes. Yes, he did. Which is why I wished to speak with you first."

"You could not wait until this evening?" He arched a dark brow. "A very good omen, my dear."

Her thin nose flared with barely restrained annoyance. "What I meant was I wished to speak with you in private."

"Ah."

"I believe there has been some dreadful misunderstanding, my lord."

"How unfortunate." Ian steepled his fingers beneath his blunt chin. "What dreadful misunderstanding are you referring to, Miss Worthington?"

She swallowed heavily as she battled her inner nerves. "My father arrived home last evening in a rather muddled state after playing cards at Lord Starner's. He claimed he lost a thousand pounds to you."

"That is true enough."

"He . . . he also claimed you offered to forgive his debt if I would become your wife."

Ian paused a long moment before giving a shrug. "It all sounds rather straightforward to me. Where is the misunderstanding?"

The green eyes widened with shock. "My lord, you could not wish to have me as a wife."

"No?" He regarded her with a mild hint of curiosity. "Is there any particular complaint that should prevent me from desiring you as Lady Barclay?"

Her lips tightened as if she sensed his inner amusement. "Several, as a matter of fact. To begin with, we are for all practical purposes strangers."

"Arranged marriages between strangers are not that uncommon. Besides, we shall obviously not be strangers for long."

His soft insinuation brought a faint color to her cheeks, but she gamely maintained her composure.

"But you know nothing about me."

"As I said, that is destined to change. Is that your only concern?"

"Certainly not." Her spine straightened as she prepared to launch her second line of defense. "I believe you should know, my lord, that I would make any gentleman a ghastly wife."

So she was going to attempt to frighten him away, he acknowledged as he lowered his hands and carefully adjusted the cuffs of his coat.

"It is true you are rather more advanced in years than the usual bride," he generously offered. "And we shall have to discuss your remarkably odd sense of fashion. But those are hardly insurmountable faults."

He heard Amanda's breath being sucked in between clenched teeth, and he glanced up to meet her glittering gaze.

"I was referring to the fact I am considered rather headstrong and set in my ways," she gritted. "Some even call me eccentric. For a goodly number of years, I have been accustomed to making my own decisions. I fear I would never be a comfortable wife."

Realizing he was supposed to be properly horrified by the image of an eccentric, headstrong countess, Ian instead smiled in a condescending fashion. He wished to keep her off guard until he had her safely wed.

"You are too hard upon yourself, Miss Worthington.

With the proper training and a firm hand, I possess every confidence that you will become a bearable wife."

"Bearable?" she demanded in dangerous tones.

"Perhaps a bit more than bearable—if you are willing to make the effort."

Her hands clenched together until the knuckles showed white. Ian could not help but admire her ability to control her smoldering temper. There were no petulant outbursts, no childish sulking or well-staged tears to sway his will. Instead she faced him squarely and offered him rational arguments. It boded well for their future, he decided. Almost as well as the distracting scent of honeysuckle he could smell from her warm skin. It made him wish he possessed the right to gather her in his arms and carry her to his bed.

Yes, the sooner they were wed the better, he acknowledged as his body stirred in reaction.

"But that is precisely my point, my lord," she retorted in tight tones, thankfully unaware of his wicked thoughts. "I have no desire to make the effort. I have no wish to marry you or any other gentleman."

Ian did not doubt her sincerity. Her father was a worthless scoundrel who had taught his daughter that gentlemen were untrustworthy, weak spirited, and utterly without morals. It would take time and patience to teach her that not all men were of the same ilk.

"That is unfortunate, of course, but hardly sensible under the circumstances. Your father was distressingly frank in his inability to meet his debt of honor. Was he mistaken?"

She paled at his soft words. "No, my father has nothing."

"Nothing but you," he pointed out gently.

Her green eyes darkened as she struggled against a

flare of panic. "Why would you desire to marry me?" she burst out. "As you so kindly pointed out, I am no longer in the fresh blush of youth, nor do I have any claim to beauty. In truth, I am an aging spinster with a shrewish tongue and managing manners."

His gaze slowly narrowed at her disparaging words. "No, my dear. You are a lady of impeccable birth who has been forced by unforgivable circumstances to take command of a faltering estate and weak-willed father. Do not fear, however. Beneath my guidance you shall soon become polished and comfortable in your role as Lady Barclay."

She appeared far from reassured by his smooth words. "You did not answer my question. Why me?"

Ian briefly wondered what she would say if he confessed he was rapidly becoming obsessed with thoughts of her, that he could not shake the vision of her seated at his table, playing chess with him by the fire, and lying in his bed.

No.

She was skittish enough as it was. Cool, detached logic was the proper method to approach her. A business arrangement, nothing more.

"You are of suitable birth. You appear to be healthy, intelligent, and you possess the sort of courage I wish to have instilled in my heirs."

"There are any number of other women who would be far more suitable than myself."

"I have no intention of returning to London and the Marriage Mart to find my bride. You will understand my reluctance to tie myself to another maiden fresh from the schoolroom."

It took a moment for her to realize he was referring to his previous fiancée, Julia Kearse. He rarely thought

of the foolish chit who had eloped with her dancing in-
structor, unless it was to breathe a prayer of gratitude at
his near miss.

"You chose me because you do not believe I will jilt
you?"

"I know you will not," he corrected softly. "You cannot afford to have a change of heart, can you, my dearest?"

"This is unbearable." She abruptly rose to her feet,
her unruly curls shimmering like gold in the October
sunlight. "I am not a piece of property to be won or lost
in a game of cards."

"Your father was willing enough to barter you in exchange for his debt."

"My father is a fool," she snapped. "I had thought
better of you."

He would give a great deal to know precisely what it
was she thought of him, Ian acknowledged ruefully. But
perhaps it was better not to know. It would no doubt
flay away any pride he might possess.

"And what have I done, beyond honoring you with
the offer of a respectable marriage?" he demanded in
reasonable tones. "It is far more than you could have
expected from any other gentleman."

A flush stained her cheeks as his shaft slid home. She
was clearly as aware as himself that her father would
have just as easily handed her over without the promise
of marriage.

"I have told you I have no desire to wed."

"You prefer living in genteel poverty, constantly fear-
ing your father will lose your home on the turn of a
card, to a position of luxury and respect as Lady
Barclay?"

An indefinable emotion rippled over her countenance. "I have lived my entire life at the mercy of my

unpredictable father," she at last said in low tones. "Now you wish me to place myself at the mercy of a stranger. All I want is to be able to control my own future. Is that really so much to ask?"

His lips twisted at her obvious frustration. She was a fool to believe she would ever be free of her father—not without his interference.

"You have forgotten the matter of your father's vowels. If I do not have you as a bride, I fear I must demand payment."

She bit her lower lip at his firm words. For a moment Ian briefly wavered. She seemed so vulnerable and alone as she stood there in the middle of the room. Then his resolve returned in full force. Amanda might not realize it at the moment, but he was doing what was best. For both of them.

"I cannot pay you today."

"Then I must insist that the marriage go forward."

She abruptly turned away, her back rigid with suppressed emotion. "If you refuse to show the least amount of mercy, may I at least request we not be wed until after Christmas?"

Ian frowned at the unexpected demand. "Why?"

"I would prefer a few weeks to become acquainted with you before the marriage."

"It will make no difference, Miss Worthington," he said in stern tones. "You will marry me."

"Then surely there can be no harm in waiting until the New Year?"

"I wish to have this business settled. I intend to return to my estates in Kent quite soon."

"Please, my lord." Slowly turning, she lowered her considerable pride to send him a pleading glance. "This will be my last Christmas with my father and friends. It will be an opportunity to say good-bye."

Ian wanted to deny her request. As he said, he wanted matters settled with as little fuss as possible. Besides, he did not entirely trust Amanda Worthington. She was far too clever and strong willed to meekly accept what fate delivered her. He did not doubt she was already scheming for some means to extract herself from the upcoming marriage.

But he was not thoroughly indifferent to her discomfort. Perhaps it would be best to give her a few weeks to accustom herself to the notion of becoming his countess, he told himself. She would realize he could be indulgent upon occasion and that he was always fair in his dealings. And certainly it would be preferable to have her come to him without the smoldering resentment he sensed beneath her careful composure.

Besides, there was no chance she could avoid the inevitable. She could not possibly possess the necessary funds to pay her father's debt. And she was far too proud to flee from her family's responsibility.

Yes, despite his own impatience to make Amanda his wife, it seemed far wiser to be generous upon this matter.

"Very well," he abruptly conceded. "We will be wed the day after Christmas."

She appeared startled by his swift concession. Then a genuine smile of relief curved her full lips.

"Thank you, my lord."

Stifling the burning ache that firmly rebelled at the mere thought of waiting so long to claim her as his own, Ian managed a gracious smile.

Soon she would be his.

Soon.

"Consider it my Christmas gift to my new fiancée."

Chapter 2

Amanda Worthington was thoroughly and gloriously
furious.

Pacing from one end of her old nurse's cramped sitting room to the other, she carefully considered the various nasty plagues she would like to have descend upon Lord Barclay.

Perhaps a painful boil upon that elegantly beautiful countenance. Or a large hump upon his broad shoulders. Or a . . . her imagination failed as she abruptly turned to retrace her steps.

Lud, was it not bad enough she had endured a lifetime of her father's foolish excesses and blithe indifference?

For as long as she could recall, she had been expected to keep their crumbling household in some semblance of order. It was her duty to ensure food was on the table and to pacify the angry tradesmen when their bills could not be paid. It was her duty to keep the manor clean when they could not afford the daily help.

Now, just when she dared to hope she had managed

to discover a measure of security for herself, Lord Barclay had snatched it away.

She did not blame her father. Well, not entirely, she amended. She had always known he was a weak, self-indulgent man who cared for nothing beyond his obsession with gambling.

But Lord Barclay.

She had thought him a cut above her father's usual cronies. He did not devote his days to gambling and hunting, nor did he litter the countryside with his illegitimate children. Instead he had concentrated his energies upon the vast estate he had purchased three years before, ensuring that it was the most efficient, most progressive land within the county. He had also revealed an unusual concern in providing his tenants with sturdy housing and enough land to keep their own stock.

In truth, Amanda had secretly admired the handsome if rather aloof earl, even if he did make her oddly uneasy whenever he was near.

Certainly she had never suspected he would be the sort of gentleman to think so poorly of women that he would be willing to barter for one in a game of chance.

A fresh wave of fury crashed through her as she clenched her hands at her sides.

She would not be traded off like an unwanted bit of property, she told herself grimly. Certainly not to a gentleman who considered her only mildly passable and chose her for the simple fact she could not say no to his proposal.

She had endured being under the rule of her father's capricious whims. She would not exchange one unbearable prison for another.

"The brute," she muttered in low tones. "The arrogant, pompous devil."

"'Ere now." An older woman with a pleasantly round face and near white hair bustled into the room, carrying a large cup that she pressed into Amanda's hands. "Have some nice hot tea. It will soothe your nerves."

Amanda grimaced at her old nurse's comforting words. Mary Brownly believed any ill in the world could be cured by a cup of tea.

"Nothing will soothe my nerves. Not unless that fiend agrees to release me from Father's promise," Amanda retorted, taking an obligatory sip of the steaming brew. She instantly coughed in shock. "Good lord, what did you put in here?"

"A tiny dollop of brandy," Mary admitted with an angelic smile. "For medicinal purposes, of course."

Amanda wiped away her tears. "More than tiny."

"Nothing like brandy to ease a heavy heart, as my pa was fond of saying."

With a shudder, Amanda set the cup aside. "I fear it will take more than brandy to ease my heart. What I need is a thousand pounds."

The old nurse dropped onto a well-padded chair. "You couldn't convince his lordship to forget your father's daft promise?"

Amanda briefly recalled the earlier encounter with Lord Barclay. How very smug he had been. So confident he could train her to be a passable countess.

Passable.

Fah.

She would rather toss herself in the nearby cove.

"No. He refused to be swayed," she said in clipped tones.

Mary heaved a sigh. "Well, perhaps it will not be so bad as you fear. He is a wealthy and titled gent. You can take your place in proper society without slaving in my kitchen every morning like a common servant. Besides, he is handsome enough to please any maiden."

Amanda shivered. "So is the devil, but I would not wish to wed him."

"My dear, he cannot be so bad."

"Really?" Amanda wrapped her arms about her waist. "Do you know the reason he wishes to make me his wife?"

Mary regarded her with a steady gaze. "No doubt because you are a beautiful maiden with a heart as large as all of England."

Amanda could not help but smile fondly at her loyal servant, the one person in the entire world who truly loved her.

"I fear it is not nearly so poetic. He wishes a lady who is completely indebted to him. One who cannot jilt him at the altar nor protest when he commands complete obedience."

Mary's expression became one of dismay at Amanda's clipped words.

"Surely you must be mistaken, my dear. Lord Barclay is well respected in the neighborhood—even by his servants, which is more than can be said of most gentlemen about here."

Amanda could not deny her claim. Unlike most gentlemen, Lord Barclay had proven to be astonishingly generous not only to his servants, but to the local village and church as well. Few commoners would not bloody the nose of anyone daring enough to speak ill of their beloved patron.

A pity he did not possess such a generous nature in regard to his future wife.

"Lord Barclay was quite clear." Her thin nose flared with distaste. "He intends to train me to be a proper wife. He will choose my clothes, polish my manners, and put a firm end to my managing nature. He has every hope that one day I shall become almost bearable."

The older woman's eyes widened in shock. "He said such a thing?"

"Yes."

Mary gave a slow shake of her head, clearly disturbed at the realization Lord Barclay could be so ruthless. "Something must be done." She banged a firm hand on the arm of her chair. "I will not have my lass treated in such an uncaring fashion. Not for all the wealth and titles in England."

Amanda fully agreed. However, it was much easier said than done. "But what?" She gave a frustrated shake of her head. "I have already sold everything from the furniture to the silver to pay Father's debts. I even sold Mother's jewelry. There is nothing left."

"That fool father of yours should be horsewhipped."

Amanda shrugged. She had lived three and twenty years with her incorrigible father, long enough to resign herself to the knowledge he would never change.

"If only I had managed to save more of the earnings we have made from our cakes," she muttered. Over five years ago, she had hit upon the notion to use her grandmother's recipe for jam cakes to make a bit of pocket money. In secrecy she had recruited Mary into her scheme, using the nurse's cottage to bake the cakes and allowing the older woman to sell them to the local bakery. Neither could have predicted just how successful the cakes would become.

Within months, local houses were demanding the cakes, as well as the local posting inn that served the numerous coaches traveling through Surrey. In time, Amanda had realized she possessed the means of salvation. No longer would she have to live her days in dread of the inevitable moment her father would lose their estate at the card table. There would be no more walking the floors at night with the knowledge she was a helpless victim to her father's fate. She could at long last take charge of her own life. With enough money, she could buy her own cottage and never again be at the mercy of another's weaknesses.

For the first time, she had possessed hope for the future.

But that had all been dashed last evening when her father had arrived home with the stunning announcement he had bartered her off like a prize horse.

Now she could not think of her cozy cottage or a life free of her father's burdens. All that mattered was avoiding marriage to Lord Barclay.

"I was forced to pay Mrs. Meeks from my savings," she continued in strained tones. "I have less than six hundred pounds left. I can never hope to earn enough to pay the debt by Christmas."

"A moment." Without warning, Mary popped to her feet and bustled across the room. Retrieving a wooden box set upon the mantel, she crossed back to Amanda and shoved it into her hands. "Here."

"What is this?"

"Over three hundred and seventy pounds I have saved."

Amanda stiffened at the generous sacrifice. "No. Absolutely not. This is for your future."

"Do not be daft. I saved this for *you*, to help with your cottage. It appears you'll be needing it sooner than I expected."

Amanda gave an adamant shake of her head. "I will not take your money."

An uncharacteristically stubborn expression settled on her round face as Mary planted her hands upon her hips. "Then you may consider it a loan."

"No, Mary."

"Amanda Worthington, I should not have a grout to

my name if not for your notion to begin our little business. More than that, you gave an old woman a joyful reason to still be alive. Without you, I should be sitting by the fire waiting to die."

Despite her best intentions, Amanda found her resolve beginning to falter. It was very tempting to think she could be so close to freeing herself from the devilish engagement.

"You have worked just as hard to make our business a success," she forced herself to point out. "This is your money."

"Yes, it is. And I can do with it what I will. I choose to give it to you." She shook a gnarled finger in Amanda's face. "No more arguments."

"Mary." Amanda gave a tremulous smile. "Thank you."

Having overcome Amanda's better sense, the wily old nurse turned her thoughts to more practical matters. "We still do not have the thousand pounds that you need."

"No, but I have convinced Lord Barclay to wait until after Christmas for our wedding," she retorted. At the moment she had pleaded to delay the marriage, she had no firm notion what she could accomplish in such a short length of time. She had known only that she had to do something. "Perhaps by then I shall have acquired what I need."

Mary gave a slow nod. "Business has been brisk of late and is bound to become even better when the gents return for the hunting season. The neighborhood will be bursting with folks."

The dark, heavy dread that had settled in Amanda's heart began to lighten. It would be difficult. To prepare and sell the number of pies she would need to raise the necessary funds was nearly mind numbing.

But anything, anything was preferable to being thrust into a cold, loveless marriage. "Yes."

"It will be hard work."

"I do not care if I must work throughout the night and day," she declared in fierce tones. "Still, we must be careful. If Lord Barclay begins to suspect what I am plotting, he might very well insist on the wedding taking place immediately."

"Aye."

Amanda furrowed her brows as she considered the dangers. She was not foolish enough to underestimate Lord Barclay. She suspected he was by far the shrewdest gentleman she had ever encountered. It would be a precarious task to disguise her scheme. "I must pretend to be resigned to my fate."

"Not too resigned, mind you," Mary cautioned. "From the local gossip, he is a clever bloke."

"As clever as Lucifer himself," Amanda agreed in dry tones. "But I must outwit him. I will not be at the mercy of yet another callous gentleman."

Mary gave a sympathetic click of her tongue as she reached out to pat Amanda's arm. "Do not fret, my dear. We will succeed."

"Yes, we will." Amanda swore in low tones. She had to hold on to some hope, she told herself, no matter how slender that hope might be. "Now I had best be on my way. Lord Barclay is expected for dinner. It will take me the entire afternoon to ensure the dining room is fit for company."

"I shall speak with the baker and see if he will be needing more cakes," Mary promised, her expression thoughtful. "I might also visit a few of the big houses and the vicarage, just to let them know we will be making an extra supply. The cooks will be happy enough to have us provide them cakes once they have a houseful of guests."

Amanda felt a wave of warmth rush through her. Mary had been the only mother she had ever known and the only person she knew she could rely upon utterly. Without her, Amanda's life would have been cold and lonely indeed.

With a swift motion, she gave the older woman a hug. "Thank you."

"Never fear." Mary laid a gentle hand upon her cheek. "We shall find a means of rescuing you from Lord Barclay."

Amanda managed a weak smile. "I pray you are right."

Chapter 3

Ian had not expected to trip over his fiancée at every turn. She certainly was not the sort to dangle after a gentleman or depend upon him to pay her incessant court. It was one of the traits that pleased him the most about Amanda Worthington.

Although he now had his estates in order and a dependable staff, he did not desire to devote his days to a demanding, vain wife. He had any number of interests he wished to pursue, and it pleased him to think Amanda could be depended upon to occupy her days in her own manner. Such an intelligent, independent woman would desire the freedom to make her plans without the constant interference of an overbearing husband.

But while he did not expect Amanda to dog his heels, he certainly had not expected her to virtually disappear.

A week after their engagement, Ian found himself in the ignoble position of lingering in a small copse of trees as he waited for Amanda to leave the cottage of her old nurse.

Dash it all, it was absurd, he told himself as his great-coat fluttered in the October breeze. He was no eager schoolboy who must skulk around in hopes of catching a glimpse of his beloved. He was a well-respected earl who expected his fiancée to be properly awaiting his arrival when he called at her home.

But while he told himself he should simply return home and sort through the large crate of plants his cousin had shipped to him from America, he found himself lingering.

He wished to see Amanda.

He wanted to enjoy her sharp-edged banter and quick wits. He wanted to see her cheeks warm with color when he became overly intimate. And he wanted to touch that satin soft skin that so haunted his dreams.

Gads, he wondered if he was becoming a bit doddy over this engagement.

Certainly his brief alliance with Julia Kearse had never created such discomfort in his life. He had asked her to wed him quite simply because she appeared to fill all his requirements for a perfect countess.

She was well bred, beautiful, young enough to bear a number of heirs, and trained from birth to be a proper bride for a titled gentleman. He had chosen her as he would choose his steward or secretary, without any serious thought that they would be bound to one another for a lifetime. He certainly hadn't wasted his days with wondering where she might be or what she might be doing, or devoted his nights to restless dreams filled with holding her in his arms.

Ian gave a shake of his head at the faint unease that flared through his heart.

Of course Amanda Worthington intruded upon his thoughts, he reassured himself. The spirited maiden was far from resigned to their engagement and no doubt searching for some means of bringing it to an end. He would be a fool not to keep her closely under guard until they were safely wed.

The closer the better, he told himself as Amanda at long last stepped from the cottage and began to make her way toward the trees. An odd tingle of anticipation spread through him as he waited for her to pass by.

Even attired in a dull gray gown and cape, there was a vivid energy about her. It was in the honey curls that peeked from beneath the ghastly bonnet and in the long, elegant movement of her stride. She was shimmeringly alive, and Ian felt his blood quicken in response.

She might not fit his youthful image of the perfect countess, but she would add a dash of spice to his life that was sadly lacking, he acknowledged.

Ian waited until she was nearly upon him before stepping from the shadows. With a swift motion he blocked the path, and Amanda was forced to come to an abrupt halt.

"My lord," she breathed, and blinked, startled.

He offered an elegant bow. "Miss Worthington."

"You frightened me."

"I apologize." Ian straightened to regard her flushed countenance. "I called at Worthington Hall, but once again I was informed you were not at home. You are very elusive, my dear."

The clear green eyes framed by a fringe of lush lashes became guarded at his soft words. "I spend every morning with my nurse, Miss Brownly."

"In the kitchen?"

She stilled at his question, an odd expression rippling over her countenance. "I beg your pardon?"

He deliberately removed his glove before reaching up to brush his fingers over her cheek. "You have flour upon your face," he said, allowing his hand to linger. Her skin was as soft and tempting as he had imagined it to be. It was an effort not to kiss her then and there.

"Oh." With a nervous motion, she stepped away from his touch. "I helped to prepare lunch for Mary."

"You must be very dedicated to your servants."

"Mary was more a mother than a servant," she retorted in defensive tones.

Ian gave a slow nod of his head. "I believe your father mentioned you lost your mother at a young age."

"I was barely three."

A flare of compassion rushed through Ian. He was well acquainted with the difficulties of being raised with a carelessly indifferent father. He knew firsthand the loneliness, the insecurity and harsh need to put aside childhood long before it was time. Like himself, Amanda had shouldered the burdens and carried them without complaint. She was well deserving of his respect.

"I myself lost my mother when I was just six. It appears we have something in common."

Their eyes briefly met in silent understanding. Then Amanda was giving a faint shake of her head. "Was there something you desired, my lord?"

His lips twisted at her instinctive retreat. Despite the fact she had agreed to their marriage, she was clearly determined to keep a distance between them.

"I believe it was your request that we become better acquainted before being wed, was it not?" he demanded, raising his brows.

She hesitated a moment before a stiff smile curved her lips. "Oh, yes. Yes, of course."

He stepped even closer, smelling the warm honey-suckle of her skin. "Oddly enough, however, while I have decided to indulge my new fiancée, I have discovered it a difficult task. You always appear to be scampering from one place to another."

A faint shiver raced through her body at his proximity. "I prefer to keep myself occupied," she said in a rather breathless voice.

"Then you are not attempting to avoid me?" he demanded.

"Certainly not."

Ian abruptly smiled in satisfaction. "Good. Then we shall spend the afternoon together."

Neatly trapped by her own words, Amanda could only give a reluctant nod of her head. "If you wish."

"I do, indeed, wish," Ian assured her with a smile.

Taking her hand, he placed it upon his arm and led her through the circle of trees. Although he was a tall gentleman, Amanda came well above his shoulder. It was a pleasant change not to have to bend down to speak with her.

Not that there was anything unfeminine about her tall, slender frame, he acknowledged. She possessed all the necessary curves to make a gentleman's thoughts turn in a dangerous direction.

Leaving the fringe of trees, he led her toward the phaeton he had left beside the road.

"Where are we going?" she demanded as he easily lifted her onto the seat.

Ian waited until he had retrieved the reins and climbed beside her before responding. "I thought you might desire to see something of your soon-to-be estate. Or at least one of your estates."

She shot him a startled gaze as they smoothly started down the road. "How many estates do you possess?"

Ian shrugged. "For the moment only this estate and my country seat in Kent. Of course, there are also my London town house and a small hunting lodge."

"Of course," she said in dry tones.

Keeping the restless bay at a sedate pace, he regarded the contrary minx in a wry fashion. "You do not appear overwhelmingly impressed by your good fortune," he retorted. "Surely you prefer the thought of residing in luxurious, well-staffed households to a crumbling manor house beyond its last prayers?"

Her expression tightened as her hands clenched together in her lap. "I shall appear an absurdity in such settings."

Ian was caught off guard by her fierce tone. Could it be she was afraid of assuming such a prominent position? It was a complication he had not predicted. "You will appear as a countess," he said firmly.

"Because Lord Barclay has proclaimed it so?" she muttered.

His lips twitched at her reference to his arrogance. He could hardly be anything but arrogant when dealing with a stubborn, sharp-tongued shrew.

"Because you are intelligent, well bred, and accustomed to running a household. With a new wardrobe and belief in yourself, you should do quite well," he stated in even tones.

"Almost bearable, in fact."

He chuckled at her swift thrust. "Without a doubt."

Her lips thinned. "That is easy for you to say. You were born to your position, not abruptly shoved into it without sufficient warning."

Ian's smile abruptly disappeared. "Nothing could be further from the truth, Miss Worthington. I may have been born to the position of earl, but I assure you it was an empty title."

"Empty?" she repeated in disbelief.

"My father was much like your own," he retorted, the very absence of emotion in his voice revealing how deeply he had been affected by the previous earl's thorough lack of morals. "He possessed little interest in his estate or those who depended upon him. He far preferred devoting his attention to such imperative matters as horse races, boxing matches, and gaming hells. Unfortunately, his lavish lifestyle far exceeded his income. It took him less than ten years to fribble away his entire fortune. It took another ten to reduce a once proud estate to ruin."

Ian's jaw clenched as he recalled the helpless fury he had experienced even as a young lad as he had watched his home stripped of his irreplaceable heirlooms and, worse, watched the tenants and servants bear the terrible brunt of his father's disinterest.

He had sworn upon his mother's grave that when he became earl, he would restore the glory that had once belonged to the Barclay family not only in the eyes of society, but among those who depended upon him for their livelihood.

He had never wavered from that promise—not when he had been forced to work long days in the fields with his tenants, not when he had climbed atop his manor house to restore the neglected roof, not when he had decided it was time to produce the necessary heir. He would not waver now. "When I came into my inheritance, there was little left beyond a derelict estate and angry tenants."

A measure of her wariness seemed to dissipate as she studied his grim countenance. "You had no income?"

"I had nothing more than two absurdly expensive

hunters and my grandmother's jewels, which I sold to finance repairs on the fields and a handful of cottages."

"I did not realize," she admitted in a low voice. "You seem to have done quite well."

"I was fortunate that my improvements swiftly made a profit and I was capable of investing for the future."

"And since then you have purchased another estate, a London town house, and a hunting lodge?"

"I wished to assure security for my tenants—and, of course, for my future heirs."

Her lashes fluttered at the mention of their children, but there was a grudging admiration in her expression she could not entirely conceal. "I would say you have succeeded in that endeavor and more. I envy your Midas touch. Thus far I have done little to halt the inevitable."

The disgust in her tone softened his features in amusement. He realized she would have felt a biting frustration as she was forced to stand aside and watch her father lose everything. For such a proud, independent woman, it must have felt like she was being slowly drowned.

That was all about to change now, he told himself, even if she did not yet realize the truth. She would soon have all the comfort and security she could ever desire. "Of course you have," he assured her. "You are marrying me."

Her green eyes flashed at his reasonable words. "That is not the same."

He shrugged. "Women are not granted the options available to gentlemen. There is nothing you could have done. It is only proper that you wed a gentleman capable of caring for your future."

Clearly unable to argue with his logic, she abruptly turned her head to offer the pure lines of her profile.

"You do realize my father will consider you his own personal banker?" she warned.

Ian had been all too aware of the danger Lord Worthington posed. He was a gentleman with no qualms whatsoever in hanging upon the coattails of his son-in-law, which was precisely why Ian had commanded his lawyer to draw up a contract that Lord Worthington would be forced to sign before the wedding.

"Your father is well aware I will offer him a monthly allowance that will keep his household in reasonable order. Any debts he incurs will be upon his own head. I will make it quite clear to all creditors that they will not be able to apply to either of us."

She gave a short, humorless laugh. "My father possesses a blithe indifference to matters of finance. He simply presumes his debts will magically disappear."

"No doubt thanks to your efforts," he retorted softly. He watched in fascination as the chilled breeze captured a golden curl to brush it over her cheek. A fierce desire to tug the horses to a halt and gather her into his arms made him grit his teeth. He could sweep her into the nearby field, he thought with a stirring pleasure, and lay her beneath him. The scent of honeysuckle would fill his senses as he drowned in her warmth.

With a wrenching effort, he damped his flare of desire, forcing himself to concentrate on their conversation. When he made this woman his own, it would be in the comfort of the wedding bed, with the entire night to ensure her pleasure, not a swift coupling to satisfy himself. "Your father will not be allowed to hide behind your skirts ever again. I shall see to that."

"Yes, I suppose," she murmured, her brows drawing together over her slender nose.

"You are frowning. Why?"

She slowly turned to meet his quizzical gaze. "I must admit I am rather puzzled."

"Why?"

"I cannot imagine that a gentleman who possesses the intelligence and ability to reclaim his inheritance is prone to making rash decisions."

"Rash?"

"Well, you can hardly claim that choosing a bride upon the turn of a card is a well-reasoned decision."

Ian could not dispute her logic. He was not the sort of gentleman who made impulsive decisions or allowed himself to be lured by the easy path. He had watched his father make a disaster of his life with such irresponsible habits. But in truth he had no rational explanation for his certainty that she was meant to be his wife. It was simply as sure as the sun rising tomorrow.

"For the most part I am a meticulous, rather tediously dull fellow. I make my plans and pursue them with hard work and determination," he admitted with a mysterious smile. "I have, however, discovered there are times when one must take a gamble upon his instincts. And my instincts tell me you will do quite well as Lady Barclay."

She regarded him for a long moment before her lips thinned. "In my experience, my lord, relying upon one's instinct is vastly overrated."

Chapter 4

Over the next two weeks, Ian remained in the annoying position of catching only the briefest glimpses of his fiancée. No matter what time he called at Worthington Hall, she was always engaged upon some activity that kept her hurrying from his side.

A slow, burning fury began to lodge itself deep within Ian. Not that he was denied the pleasure of Amanda's company, although he did long for a few hours of uninterrupted conversation with his intended, but because he could detect the burgeoning traces of utter exhaustion upon the young maiden.

With each passing day, she appeared to become thinner and thinner, with deepening shadows beneath those magnificent eyes. She was as fragile as the finest crystal, and he very much feared she might suddenly shatter.

Arriving at Worthington Hall the first week in November, Ian reached the limit of his temper. With no one to answer his summons at the door yet again, he had let himself in and gone in search of Amanda. He

His silver eyes hardened to tempered steel as Ian regarded his future father-in-law. "So good, in fact, that you sold her to save your own hide."

There was a shocked silence before Lord Worthington clenched his hands in anger. Ian could detect no remorse in the pale blue eyes, only a petulant embarrassment at being chastised by a gentleman considerably younger than himself.

"You were willing enough to buy," he accused.

Just for the briefest moment, Ian felt a twinge of guilt. He could not deny he had been eager to use Lord Worthington's lack of morals to his own advantage. He had wanted Amanda. It had not mattered how he acquired his goal.

Then he was swiftly thrusting aside his rare disquiet. What he had done was as much for Amanda as himself. "I assure you she will receive the utmost care and consideration as my wife. Far more than she was offered beneath your roof."

Lord Worthington shot him a sour glare. "You might think differently when you have endured the sharp edge of her tongue," he warned in peevish tones. Then, suddenly realizing what he had said, his face paled. "Not that she isn't a fine maiden, mind you. As fine as they come."

Ian's lips thinned with impatience. Lord Worthington would never change, no matter how many lectures.

"I did not seek you out to discuss Miss Worthington's tongue."

"No?" The older gentleman licked his lips with a hint of wariness. "You haven't had a change of heart, have you? I must remind you we have a gentleman's agreement."

"No, I have not had a change of heart," Ian retorted in sharp tones. "Indeed, I am extremely anxious to remove Amanda from this household. Until then, however, I will not allow my fiancée to be treated as the hired help. Tomorrow morning I will begin to interview staff for Worthington Hall. If I discover Amanda has so much as darned a hem after today, you shall answer to me." His silver eyes narrowed. "Do you understand?"

There was a moment's pause as Lord Worthington battled between pride and greed. Predictably his greed swiftly won out, and a smile returned to his lips.

"Yes, certainly. Most generous of you."

"I do this for Amanda," Ian retorted in stern tones.

Not waiting for the older gentleman's response, Ian turned about and left the library. Gads, he longed to have the man strung up and horsewhipped. Only the knowledge that such a delightful pastime would accomplish nothing more than to embarrass Amanda kept him grimly headed back to the parlor.

Soon Amanda would be free of her father, he assured himself. Never again would she be treated as a servant or bartered to pay off debts. She would be safe.

He did not pause to consider why he trembled with fury at the thought of Amanda being reared with such callous disregard. Perhaps it echoed too closely his own childhood. Or perhaps he simply realized Amanda's natural distrust of men was bound to make their relationship difficult. He only knew he wished to sweep her from this crumbling house and place her close to his side.

Entering the parlor, he discovered Amanda just struggling to a sitting position. Ian smiled as he crossed to retrieve his coat and toss it onto a nearby chair. With her face still flushed with sleep and her honey curls tumbled, she appeared closer to twelve than three and twenty.

"My lord," she murmured, attempting to clear her foggy thoughts as he settled close beside her.

"Good afternoon, my dear."

"I did not realize you had arrived."

"No." His lips twisted. "You were clearly exhausted."

Her expression became oddly guarded at his soft words. "I fear I have not been sleeping well."

Ian wondered if she thought him unaware of the burdens she shouldered. Reaching out, he briefly stroked her reddened fingers. "It is more than a lack of sleep that has you exhausted."

She swiftly attempted to hide her hands in the folds of her faded brown gown. "It is nothing."

Ian abruptly frowned. "It is insupportable. From this day forward, you may be assured there will be adequate staff to see to your needs."

Amanda blinked in confusion. "What?"

"My secretary will ensure that the necessary servants are hired, beginning tomorrow."

"But we cannot pay the wages . . ."

His hand once again reached out, this time to press his fingers to the softness of her lips. "I will see to the wages."

Her eyes widened—whether at his offer or at the feel of his fingers, which moved to trace the line of her jaw, Ian could not determine.

"Why?"

"You deserve better," he said simply, distracted by the warm silk of her skin.

"I would prefer you did not," she stubbornly argued.

"You are my fiancée. I wish to ensure your welfare."

"I am quite well."

"Indeed." His hand moved to lightly grasp her chin. He tilted her chin up until she was forced to meet his steady regard. "You are so thin I fear you might disappear in a wisp of smoke. And each day those shadows beneath your eyes become more pronounced. I do not wish the neighborhood to fear I mistreat you."

Her long lashes fluttered downward in charming confusion. "No one would believe such a thing."

Ian instinctively scooted closer, bewitched by the warm scent of honeysuckle clouding his senses. "I certainly hope not." His hand cupped her cheek as his blood heated in a dangerous fashion. "I intend to take excellent care of you, Miss Worthington."

Easily sensing the sudden tension in the air, Amanda lifted her gaze in wary unease. "My lord."

"Your skin is like the finest silk," he murmured huskily. "Gads, but you enchant me."

Although a gentleman of considerable restraint, Ian had devoted too many sleepless nights to battling his desire to resist such temptation. She was so close, her lips already parted as if in anticipation of his touch.

With a small groan Ian slowly lowered his head and captured her mouth in a kiss of sweet possession.

They both froze as their lips made contact, momentarily shocked, as a bolt of lightning seemed to strike between them. Sizzling heat and breathless anticipation shimmered in the air, making Ian tremble at the tidal force of delight that surged through his body.

Dear lord, he had expected to enjoy kissing this woman, he thought in dizzy pleasure, but he had not expected to have his breath stolen and his heart halted by a mere kiss.

Threading his fingers into her soft curls, he drank deeply of her innocence. She shivered beneath his demands, then hesitantly leaned closer to his taut form. Ian felt a sharp tingle of excitement flood through his body. She was not indifferent to him, he acknowledged with a low growl of satisfaction. This delectable ache clutching deep within him was echoed in her own tentative response.

Easing the demands of his kiss, he pressed tender, impatient kisses over her cheek and down the curve of her neck. When he reached the frantic pulse at the base of her throat, Amanda gave a small jolt of surprise. "Oh."

With a low chuckle Ian pulled back to regard her bemused expression. "What is it, Miss Worthington?"

Her green eyes glittered with the brilliance of emeralds. "I have never been kissed before."

A startling burst of masculine satisfaction filled his heart at her shaky confession. "That is fortunate."

"Why?"

"Because I believe I might strangle any man who had touched you. You are mine, Miss Worthington. Now and forever."

He reached down to place a swift, branding kiss upon her lips.

She gazed at him for a long, bewildered moment. Then she gave a sharp shake of her head. "I do not believe this is entirely proper, my lord."

"We are engaged," he reminded her softly.

"But not yet wed."

His body throbbed with need as his gaze lowered to her lips still swollen from his kisses. "That could easily be changed."

Without warning, she stiffened in panic. "No, you promised we would wed after Christmas."

Ian discovered himself annoyed by her fierce refusal. Blast it all. Why did she hesitate? He could offer her all a maiden could desire: A title, beautiful homes, well-trained servants, a prominent position among society and nights filled with passion.

Surely such a life was preferable to the dreary drudgery beneath her father's roof?

Meeting her wide emerald gaze, Ian heaved a resigned sigh. She still did not trust him, he realized with an odd pang of disappointment. "Very well. I shall attempt to be patient," he agreed in low tones. "In the meantime, you are to rest and regain your strength. I will not have my bride fainting at the altar."

Her head ducked as she studied her tightly clenched fingers. "I can safely assure you that will not occur, my lord."

Ian stilled, not at all certain he trusted her strange promise. His instincts urged him to toss her over his shoulder and carry her off before she could slip away.

Unfortunately, he had given his word, he reminded himself grimly. There was nothing he could do but bide his time.

Ian rose to his feet, regarding her bent head with a mixture of lingering desire and frustration. "I shall see to it, my dear."

"Yes," she murmured, clearly waiting for him to take his leave.

With a faint shake of his head, Ian retrieved his coat and walked from the room. Perhaps one day he would comprehend his elusive, maddening fiancée. For now, however, it appeared he would have to remain patient.

Thankfully, that was a skill he had developed at a very young age.

Still reeling in shock, Amanda vaguely realized Lord Barclay had left the room.

She felt as if she had just been dropped from the top

of a high cliff. Raising trembling fingers, she pressed her lips, which still tingled from Lord Barclay's kiss.

Dear heavens, she had never expected to feel such pleasure from the mere pressing of lips together. In truth, she had expected to feel nothing but revulsion if ever forced to endure the advances of her fiancé.

Instead she had felt scalded with a magical heat that had made her long to press closer. She had wanted to discover more of the delightful sensations. To feel his hands upon her . . .

Amanda shuddered as she realized she had just experienced her first taste of desire.

It had been a potent, frightening, rather wonderful experience.

And it must never, ever happen again, she told herself sternly. Abruptly rising to her feet, Amanda came to the firm decision she needed to find some means of distracting her disturbing thoughts.

She had taken no more than a step, however, when her father charged into the room wearing a petulant frown. "There you are, Amanda."

Amanda heaved a frustrated sigh. She was in no humor for one of Lord Worthington's sulks. "Yes, Father?"

"Has the wretched upstart taken his leave?"

"If you are referring to Lord Barclay, then yes," she retorted, puzzled by her father's peculiar reference to his latest patron. Until this moment, Lord Barclay had been nothing less than a saint.

"The blasted audacity of the cur. To lecture me as if I were a . . . well, no matter." Determinedly patting his cravat, her father gave a small sniff. "At least we shall have a decent staff."

Amanda experienced a sharp flare of embarrassment. "Paid for by Lord Barclay," she retorted bitterly.

Lord Worthington shrugged. "And why not? We are family now, after all."

Amanda clenched her teeth in grim exasperation. "Not yet, Father. And I'll thank you not to forget it."

"What the devil is that supposed to mean?"

"It means any number of things could occur before our wedding," she warned. "Not the least of which is Lord Barclay realizing that having a sharp-tongued spinster as a wife and a father-in-law constantly on the dun is the very last thing he desires."

Her father swallowed heavily. "He wouldn't."

She gave a hollow laugh. "Only if he possesses the least amount of sense."

Chapter 5

Amanda regarded the small, birdlike woman standing in her drawing room as if she were a spawn of the devil.

It had been bad enough to awaken this morning to discover a steady stream of servants taking their place within the household—a new housekeeper, two maids, and a footman thus far. But to discover the local dressmaker awaiting her directly after breakfast had been more than she could bear.

Dear heavens, does Lord Barclay think he can simply step into my life and take total command? she had seethed in frustration. Did he not consider she possessed any sensibilities at all?

But even as the thoughts had flashed through her mind, Amanda had known she was not truly offended by Lord Barclay's interference in her life.

Certainly he possessed his share of arrogance and was far too fond of having his own way. But the knowledge that he had been acting out of consideration for her had kept her pacing the floor though the long night.

For the first time in her life, Amanda was confronted by a gentleman who genuinely saw her as a woman. He noticed her clothes were shabby and that she could barely keep her eyes open after ensuring her father was fed a decent breakfast.

How was he to know her weariness was more a result of rising at three to bake jam cakes so she could end their engagement rather than keeping her household from ruin?

And now he had sent the dressmaker to provide all the gowns she had ever dreamed of possessing. It made her gut twist with inner guilt. She could bear anything from Lord Barclay—anything but his kindness.

Tilting her chin to a defensive angle, Amanda wrapped her arms about her waist. "No. Absolutely not," she stated in firm tones.

The tiny seamstress regarded her with growing dismay. "But, Miss Worthington, I was instructed to take your measurements. I promise you it won't take a moment of your time."

"And I am instructing you to return to your shop. I have no need for new gowns."

With a frown, the woman allowed her gaze to briefly survey the threadbare gray gown that was far too tight over Amanda's bosom and two inches too short.

"Surely you'll be wanting at least one special gown for your wedding?" she coaxed, clearly disappointed at the thought of losing such a profitable opportunity. "Every maiden wishes to appear lovely on such a special day."

A peculiar, wholly unexpected pang clutched at Amanda's heart. "No."

"But . . ."

"Thank you, Mrs. White, that will be all for now," a dark, masculine voice commanded from the doorway.

Both women turned to discover Lord Barclay stepping into the room. Amanda's breath caught at the sight of his tall form, attired in a dark gold coat and buff breeches.

It was not only his thoughtful generosity that had kept her awake during the night, she reluctantly conceded, but the memory of his provocative kisses.

Kisses she already longed to taste again.

With an effort, she hid her confusion behind a mask of cold composure. In contrast, the seamstress sank into a desolate curtsy as she realized she was not about to receive her large commission. "Yes, sir."

Silence reined as the older woman left the room. Then, with a watchful gaze, Lord Barclay crossed toward Amanda's stiff form. "Good morning, my dear."

"Lord Barclay."

His lips twitched with a rueful humor as he noted her tight expression. "I suppose I need not inquire how you are feeling on this fine day."

Amanda refused to respond to his potent charm. Lud, he was as dangerous as a stalking tiger. "Did you request Mrs. White to call upon me?"

"Yes." He lifted one broad shoulder. "Obviously not one of my better notions."

She forced herself to meet his narrowed silver gaze. "I am not yet your wife, to be clothed at your whim. If I am an embarrassment in my faded gowns, then you are welcome to cry off."

His smile abruptly faded at her sharp words. With a deliberate motion he stepped close enough to cloak her in the heat of his powerful body. "I asked Mrs. White to come this morning because I thought you would be pleased to have a few fashionable gowns. You have never been and will never be an embarrassment to me, Miss Worthington. Indeed, I feel nothing but pride at the knowledge you will soon be my countess. Now I suggest you sheath that sharp tongue before you truly rile my temper."

Amanda abruptly lowered her lashes, assaulted by yet another pang of guilt. Dash it all, why could he not remain the cold, aloof earl she had thought him to be? It would be far more comfortable to deceive such a gentleman than one who displayed nothing but kind concern for her welfare. "I am sorry, my lord, but it is hardly proper for you to be purchasing my wardrobe," she forced herself to murmur.

"I believed you were impervious to local gossip."

She grimaced at the realization he knew her far too well. "I am not referring to the local rattles," she corrected in low tones. "I may not have much else, but I do have my pride. You have insisted on providing Worthington Hall with servants. I will not also be indebted for the clothes on my back."

"How can you speak of debt? You will soon be my wife. What is mine is now yours."

Amanda's gaze flew upward in instinctive protest. "Not yet."

He shrugged. "A few weeks can hardly signify."

"It does to me." She drew in a deep breath and condemned her prickly pride to the devil. "Please, my lord."

For a long, nerve-wracking moment he studied her pale features with a fierce intensity, almost as if he sought to discover the secrets she harbored deep within. Then her heart gave a sharp twinge as a smile slowly curved his sculptured lips. "Very well, Miss Worthington. I once again bow to your wishes. You see what an indulgent husband I shall be?"

She shivered—whether from fear or some more potent emotion, she refused to consider. "Thank you, my lord."

"I only wish to make you at ease in your new position," he said softly. "Hardly an unforgivable sin, is it, my dear?"

"No, of course not," she retorted in weak tones.

"Good. Then perhaps you could bring yourself to call me Ian?"

"If you wish," she conceded reluctantly.

Without warning, his hand lifted to gently brush a wayward curl that had already escaped her tidy knot. "What extraordinary hair you possess, my dear." His voice was suddenly husky. "Was it a gift from your mother?"

Amanda struggled to breathe. "My grandmother. She was from Scotland."

He gave a low chuckle. "Ah, that explains your rather stubborn nature."

A seductive magic was beginning to weave its way through Amanda. She wanted to lean forward and press herself to that hard form. She wanted to be swept into his arms and carried to her room.

It was all wickedly confusing. "Ian."

He smiled deep into her eyes as if sensing her uncertainty. "Yes, Amanda?"

She struggled to regain control of her rattled senses. "Was there something you desired?"

His silver eyes flared at her unwittingly provocative question. "Yes, there is something I desire very much," he murmured. Holding her wide gaze, he lowered his dark head and captured her mouth in a soft, seeking kiss that made her toes curl with pleasure. For a breathless moment, his lips tasted and teased her own before he slowly pulled back to regard her bemused expression. "I have been longing to do that again since yesterday. I do not believe I slept at all last night recalling the soft sweetness of those lips."

A hectic blush filled her cheeks at the thought of this gentleman experiencing the same dazzling desire as herself. It forged a bond of intimacy that was deeply disturbing. "Oh."

He regarded her flushed cheeks with a searching gaze. "Tell me, Amanda, do you fear the marriage bed?"

Amanda was caught off guard by the blunt question. "I . . . I have not given it much thought."

His fingers gently brushed her trembling lips. "It would not be unusual if you did. Most innocents do, especially those with no mother to comfort them. I assure you, however, that you need not be apprehensive. I shall take matters at a pace that will bring you only pleasure."

The heat that had pooled deep in her stomach flamed with a sudden life. Amanda knew what she felt at the thought of sharing a marriage bed with this man was not fear. It was far closer to a shameful need as unnerving as it was unexpected. "My lord."

"Ian," he corrected firmly.

"Ian." She gave an unconscious shake of her head, hoping to clear her foggy mind. "I would rather not discuss such a subject."

His brows drew together in a faint frown. "I do not mean to embarrass you. But I would not have you come to this marriage with fear of me."

"I do not fear you," she protested.

"Then why are you so wary when I am near?"

"It is not often that I discover myself engaged," she attempted to defend herself. "I think it is only to be expected that I am somewhat wary."

"You have been wary of me since I first arrived in Surrey," he charged.

She bit her bottom lip at his aggravating perception. "That is not true."

"Yes, it is, even if you are too stubborn to admit it," he continued with a relentless persistence. "And I believe I know why."

Her heart skipped a beat. "Really?"

He shifted his hand to grasp her chin. "Yes. You are accustomed to keeping others at bay with that frightful tongue and efficient manner, but I refuse to be bullied. You cannot hide from me."

Amanda abruptly stepped from his distracting touch. She did not want to admit he was right. To acknowledge she had instinctively feared he could arouse the unfamiliar sensations of desire within her only made her feel more vulnerable. "That is absurd."

His rather mocking smile assured her he was not deceived for a moment. Thankfully, however, he seemed content to allow her a measure of dignity.

Stealing a sweet, bone melting kiss, he offered her a half bow.

"I shall call upon you later, my dearest."

Chapter 6

Nearly a week later, Ian surveyed the large ballroom in the east wing of his home. Although he had naturally examined the entire estate before making his purchase, he had not returned to this distant wing since taking possession of the house.

He felt a measure of satisfaction now as he noted the large, lofty proportions and formal chandeliers. It could not compare with the vast ballroom at his country seat in Kent, he acknowledged, but there was a decided charm to the gilt moldings and green satin wall coverings. Not even the cupids that dotted the ceiling could be wholly condemned.

In his mind he pictured the dust covers removed and a large crowd of glittering guests waltzing beneath the candlelight. Amanda would be upon his arm as they stood at the doorway, or perhaps joined the dancers upon the floor. A small, pleased smile curved his lips.

He was uncertain when the notion of hosting a Yuletide Ball had struck him. He only knew he longed to lay public claim to Amanda Worthington, to brand her as his own before every neighbor in the county. Perhaps then he would rid himself of the nagging concern she might somehow slip from his grasp.

With a faint shake of his head at his odd fancy, Ian turned to regard the slim, fair-haired man standing at his side. Peter Broom had been his secretary for the past five years. A quiet, unassuming gentleman, he managed Ian's affairs with a ruthless efficiency. There was no task too minor or too difficult to be accomplished. Ian had long ago given up attempting to discover the young man's method of procuring his favorite brandy, of ensuring he was never bothered by unwelcome interlopers, and of keeping his accounts in perfect order. He only knew he could leave the details of the ball in the young gentleman's capable hands without hesitation.

"Yes, this will do nicely," he announced, his hands planted upon his hips. "Have Mrs. Warren hire whatever help she needs from the village to have the room made presentable."

Peter scribbled a note upon the sheet of paper he carried with him. "Yes, my lord."

"We shall need musicians, of course, and order the champagne from London. The food I shall leave in your hands." Ian glanced once again across the long room. "We should also consider some sort of decorations. Perhaps some holly and fir for the Christmas season."

"And mistletoe," Peter added with a perfectly straight face.

Ian felt a delicious heat shimmer through him. The memory of Amanda's kisses was never far from his mind. In truth, the image of holding her slender frame in his arms intruded into his thoughts with such increasing frequency he found it difficult to concentrate on anything else.

Strangely, however, he had given up his resentment over the unexplainable obsession he felt for Amanda Worthington. It might not be reasonable, or even sensible, but it was undeniable.

He might as well attempt to stop the beat of his heart as to put Amanda from his thoughts.

"Ah yes, plenty of mistletoe," he agreed, a glow of anticipation in his silver eyes. "You will see to the invitations?"

"Of course."

"We shall also have to consider a less formal entertainment for the tenants. They will no doubt wish to celebrate my upcoming marriage."

Peter glanced up to offer Ian a faint smile. "They are all very pleased, if I may be so bold as to say so."

"They approve of my choice in brides?" Ian demanded.

"Very much. Miss Worthington is well liked throughout the county."

Ian smiled in contentment. Unlike his irresponsible father, he concerned himself deeply with the happiness of those who depended upon him. Although his first fiancée had been chosen to impress those among society, he was far more pleased now to realize his bride would be respected among the tenants and staff. Any woman with the proper clothes and title of countess would be accepted among society. It would take a woman of genuine loyalty and kindness to be accepted by his tenants.

The image of a pale countenance with flashing green eyes and curls as golden as a setting sun rose to his mind. "She will not be a comfortable wife, I fear," he admitted in wry tones.

Peter gave a chuckle, obviously familiar with Miss Worthington's stubborn nature.

"No, she is a rather strong-willed maiden."

Ian grimaced. "She is a fiery shrew who will no doubt lead me a merry chase, but I believe she will make a fine countess."

"Yes."

Still pondering the elusive, unpredictable woman he was about to make his wife, Ian was struck by a sudden thought. "Oh, I nearly forgot. Did you send a groom to Kent for my mother's jewels?"

"Yes, he returned yesterday. I locked them in your desk."

Ian felt a surge of impatience. He wished to place an engagement ring upon Amanda's finger as swiftly as possible. It would be yet another means of publicly binding her to him. All would know that soon she would be Lady Barclay, especially Amanda herself.

"Let us have a look at them," he retorted, already leaving the ballroom and marching back to the main house. Peter hurried behind, his shorter stride making him nearly gallop to keep pace. In short order, Ian entered his study and, removing the key from his pocket, he unlocked the lower drawer. He easily discovered the rosewood box and set it atop the desk. "Here we are."

Flipping open the box, he examined the handful of gems with a tiny pang. The glorious Barclay diamonds, and even his mother's personal rubies, had been sold by his father long ago. There were pitifully few jewels of any value left.

For a moment Ian battled the familiar surge of anger at his father's extravagance. Amanda would have looked stunning in his mother's rubies. How they would have sparkled upon her satin skin, tantalizing flames against the whiteness. Then he gave a sharp shake of his head.

One day he would buy Amanda all the diamonds and rubies she desired. For now he sought a simple symbol of their bond.

Sorting through the few pearl necklaces and plain brooches, Ian at last discovered what he was searching for. His anger dissolved as he pulled out a delicate silver ring with a small emerald surrounded by diamonds.

He held it into the light and Peter gave a nod of his head as the emerald sparkled to life. "It is lovely."

"It belonged to my grandmother," Ian explained with an unconscious smile. Although the old woman could be a frightening tartar when she chose, Ian had adored her. It had been a painful wrench when she had died. "I fear the setting is rather old fashioned."

"Do you wish me to take it to London and have it reset?"

"No." Ian gave a decisive shake of his head. "If Miss Worthington does not care for it, I will purchase her another. I was unable to save many heirlooms from my father's excesses. I prefer to retain the few I still possess."

All too familiar with the previous earl's habit of selling whatever he could lay his hands upon, Peter offered a smile of sympathy. "Of course."

Ian's lips twitched. "Besides, I wish to see it upon her finger. She reminds me a great deal of the old dragon." Abruptly pushing the ring into his pocket, Ian once again experienced that sharp surge of impatience. "That will be all for now, Peter. I believe I shall call upon Miss Worthington."

The younger man hastily dipped his head, but not before Ian noted the pleased glow that entered his eyes.

"Very good."

Ian hesitated a moment, wondering if he were making a fool of himself. For the past week he had devoted himself to procuring trained servants for Worthington

Hall, refurbishing the bedchamber that would be Amanda's, and mooning over plans for a Yuletide Ball. And now, when he should be concerned with the new roof being placed upon the stables, he was instead anxious to rush to Worthington Hall and place his ring upon Amanda's finger.

Surely it was not the behavior of a gentleman who had chosen his bride for sensible, utterly logical reasons?

He wavered between common sense and the tingling urge to visit Amanda before giving a restless shrug. He could not possibly concentrate upon the blasted roof when his thoughts were consumed with the image of slipping his ring upon Amanda's finger. It was best simply to be done with the task so he could return and tend to his own duties.

Having come to his decision, Ian wasted no time. Within an hour he was standing in Worthington Hall's foyer, regarding the ancient butler he had personally ensured was delivered from Kent. "Ah, Forrest, how does it go?" he inquired as he handed over his greatcoat and hat.

Clearly pleased to see his benefactor, the servant offered a dignified bow. "Very well, my lord. I must thank you for offering me a post here. It was a rare disappointment to have lost my position at the Hogans'."

Ian considered it a stroke of fortune to have discovered his neighbors in Kent had recently retired their butler in favor of an African servant complete with turban.

"I am the one who should thank you for arriving so swiftly. Butlers with your skills are not easy to come by."

Forrest heaved a sigh. "I fear servants such as myself are swiftly growing out of fashion, my lord."

"Only to those fools who care more for shocking

their guests than seeing to their comfort," he assured the older man.

"Thank you, sir."

"Is Miss Worthington about?"

"I believe she is in the library."

"I shall show myself in."

Forrest gave a nod of his head. "Very good."

Making his way up the broad staircase, Ian was pleased to note the freshly polished wood and scent of beeswax in the air. Already the house was losing its dusty air of neglect and gleaming with a new life. He could even detect the tantalizing aroma of freshly baked bread wafting from the kitchen.

He hoped good food and a measure of rest would restore Amanda's fragile stamina. It was uncomfortably painful to see her so pale and thin.

Entering the library, he discovered Amanda seated at the heavy desk. A satisfied smile curved his lips as he realized she did appear to have some color in her cheeks, even though she was still entirely too slender.

"Good afternoon, Amanda."

At the sound of his voice, Amanda jerked her head upward. Then, surprisingly, she hastily swept a handful of coins from the desk and into a drawer that she shut with a bang.

"Ian," she breathed as she awkwardly rose to her feet.

Ian paused, not caring for the notion that his intended possessed anything she felt in need of hiding from him. "Am I intruding?" he demanded.

"Of course not." She moved around the desk, pushing away the stray curls that had tumbled about her face. "I was just balancing the household accounts."

Ian was far from convinced. There had been something very furtive about her reaction to his sudden presence. Still, he could not force her to confess what she had been about, he ruefully acknowledged. She was far too stubborn to be coerced.

Unconsciously reaching into his pocket, Ian grasped his fingers about his grandmother's ring. The sooner he had this woman bound to him the better, he grimly decided. "Rather a tedious means of spending the day," he offered in smooth tones.

"I do not mind." She gave a vague shrug. "Indeed, it is the only task I am allowed to perform these days. I cannot even walk across the room without tripping over someone in their rush to open the door."

His smile returned at her dry tone. Miss Amanda Worthington was accustomed to being in charge. It would be difficult for her to accept she was no longer needed to keep the household in order.

"Good. You appear considerably more well rested. In truth, you look quite beautiful."

She cast a deliberate glance at her ill-fitted gown. "You did not take a fall and bump your head on the way over, did you?"

"No. My faculties are quite unimpaired, my dear," he assured her. "I am simply capable of seeing beyond a well-worn gown."

A hint of confusion entered her eyes at his soft words. "Was there something you needed?"

"I called because I have a small token I wished to give you."

She abruptly stiffened. "Oh no, please. I do not wish anything."

Ian's lips twisted. "Do not fear. I have learned my lesson in overstepping the bounds of propriety. This is perfectly acceptable for a gentleman to offer his fiancée."

"What is it?"

Slowly withdrawing his hand from his pocket, Ian opened his fingers to reveal the delicate ring. "It belonged to my grandmother."

"Oh."

"Do you like it?"

There was no mistaking the genuine pleasure that glowed in her eyes. "It is lovely."

An odd, unexpected burst of warmth spread through Ian's heart. Amanda was perhaps the only woman in England who would prefer the understated elegance of the ring to a more gaudy display of wealth.

"Here. Allow me to put it on," he said, grasping her hand and firmly sliding the ring onto her finger. It looked as beautiful as he had hoped, he acknowledged, lifting her fingers to his lips. "Perfect."

Without warning she abruptly snatched her hand free, her eyes wide with unmistakable panic. "I cannot accept this."

Ian frowned at her absurd reaction. Gads, would he ever comprehend this maddening woman?

"Of course you can. There is nothing improper in an engagement ring."

She licked her lips in a nervous manner. "But it is your grandmother's."

"Which is precisely why I wish you to have it," he said in firm tones. "You are a great deal like her. Impertinent, independent, and quite delightful."

Perversely his words of comfort only managed to deepen her agitation. Clutching her hands together, she jerkily turned away from him. "I cannot. I . . . I might lose it."

Ian's frown deepened as he stepped forward and placed his hands upon her shoulders. His touch held a measure of male possession as well as an unspoken warning. "You will not lose it, Amanda, and even if you did I would simply buy you another. That ring symbolizes the fact that you are mine. There is no escape."

He felt her shudder beneath his fingers.

Chapter 7

For once it was not difficult for Amanda to rise at the unreasonable hour of three in the morning—not because she had been relieved of performing the slightest duty about Worthington Hall, although she could not deny a vast pleasure in not constantly fretting over the endless chores, but because she had not been able to close her eyes the entire night.

Ignoring the sharp chill in the air, Amanda hastily washed and dressed in a heavy wool gown. Then, cautiously slipping from the slumbering house, she made her way to Mary's small cottage.

As always, her old servant already had the oven warming and the cabinets cluttered with the ingredients Amanda used to create her jam cakes. Tossing off her thick cape, she ignored the long list of orders Mary held in her hand and instead wrapped her arms about her waist as she stood in the middle of the room.

"Oh, Mary, it is all so horrid," she burst out, allowing the festering guilt to wash through her with painful intensity.

Instantly concerned, Mary dropped the list and hurried to her side.

"What is it, my child? Your father, I suppose?" she demanded.

Amanda grimaced, realizing that for once her troubles had nothing to do with her father. At least not entirely. She could not avoid shouldering her own measure of blame on this occasion. "No, it is Lord Barclay."

The older woman gave a startled blink. "What has he done?"

Biting her lower lip, Amanda abruptly thrust out her hand to reveal the delicate emerald ring. "He gave me this."

Mary carefully studied the ring that seemed to sear Amanda's very skin with shame. "Well, it is a mite old fashioned, but lovely nonetheless." Her nurse at last lifted her puzzled gaze. "You do not care for it?"

Amanda gave an impatient click of her tongue. "Of course I care for it. It is beautiful."

"Then what ails you?"

Her eyes darkened with her tangled emotions. "I feel like a traitor. I am wearing Lord Barclay's ring while all along I am attempting to end this engagement."

"Ah," Mary breathed in sudden comprehension.

With a shake of her head Amanda restlessly paced across the cramped kitchen.

"It all seemed so simple when he forced me into this engagement," she muttered. "He was so cold, so clearly indifferent to my own feelings at being thrust into marriage. What could I do but find a means of freeing myself from such an unbearable situation?"

"Yes, indeed," the old nurse dutifully agreed. "Quite understandable."

"No maiden could be expected to simply allow herself to be handed over like a parcel of property. It is barbaric."

"Barbaric."

Amanda heaved a harsh breath. The excuses she had muttered to herself over and over through the long night were beginning to sound empty even to her ears. "If only he would halt being so bloody kind," she ground out in frustration.

"Yes, well, I suppose it was kind to offer his grandmother's ring," Mary retorted, clearly confused by Amanda's obvious distress.

No more confused than herself, Amanda wryly admitted, turning back to retrace her steps. "It is not just the ring. It is filling the house with servants because I look weary. And commanding Mrs. White to create me a new wardrobe so I would feel more at ease in my new position." She came to a halt, her features tightening with a flare of pain. "Do you know what he said to me?"

"What?"

"That he was proud at the thought of having me as his countess."

"And well he should be," Mary loyally retorted. "You would make a fine countess."

Amanda pressed a hand to her stomach that felt as if it were tied in knots. Of course Mary did not comprehend her uncertain emotions. She had always been careful to pretend a thorough indifference to her father's lack of affection. Even when she was very young, she had appeared briskly competent and quite above any childish need for approval.

Only in the deepest, darkest part of her did she ever allow herself to harbor the yearning that someday she would discover someone to love and appreciate her. How would it feel to have someone's eyes light up when she entered a room? Or to have strong arms hold her close when she was sad? They were dangerous emotions that she had kept well secluded.

Until Lord Barclay had stormed into her life.

Suddenly she felt as if her secret desires had been stripped bare, leaving her vulnerable to the needs she had so long denied. Realizing that Mary was regarding her with a gathering concern, Amanda managed a weak smile. "No one has ever told me they were proud of me before."

Moving forward, Mary laid a hand upon her arm. "Are you having second thoughts, my child?"

Amanda gave a restless shrug. "I do not know what my thoughts are at present. It is all so vastly confusing."

"You know, Amanda, a maiden could do worse than wed a gentleman who is so considerate," Mary said with a speculative gleam in her faded eyes.

Amanda caught her breath at the blunt suggestion. Marry Lord Barclay?

Her heart nearly halted at the mere notion.

Not that she any longer feared he would be cruel or even indifferent to her. Indeed, he had proven to be far more considerate and gentle than she could ever have dreamed possible. And the thought of being held in his arms and sharing his bed made the most wickedly pleasant sensations course through her blood.

But while she no longer feared Lord Barclay, she shuddered at the thought of being bound to him for life. "No. It is impossible."

Detecting the edge in her voice, Mary frowned in puzzlement. "What is it?"

Amanda paused for a long moment. Almost inconsequentially, she noted the faint crackle of the fire and the scent of dried herbs that filled the air. There was a comfortable feel of home in the small, sparse cottage. A feeling she could breathe easily and simply be herself. It was a feeling that had always been absent from Worthington Hall.

This was what she wanted for her future—a place she could call home.

"I want more," she said softly.

"What do you mean?"

Amanda spread her hands as she sought the words to express her coiled thoughts. "I have lived all my life knowing that my father tolerated me because I could keep his household in order. I do not wish to go to another household where I am wanted only because I am convenient and do not remind Lord Barclay of his previous fiancée. I want to be wanted for myself. Not to fulfill someone else's needs."

Mary studied her for a long moment. Then a sad smile curved her lips. "Do you love him, my dear?"

Oddly Amanda was not shocked by the ludicrous question. Although she had refused to give a name to the warm sensations that washed through her at the thought of Lord Barclay, she had known all along they were perilous.

Slowly but surely, he had tunneled his way into her heart, slipping through the walls of defense she had worked so hard to build.

"I do not know," she painfully admitted. "He is so much different than I thought him to be. He can be arrogant, but he is also kind and generous. And I do not believe I have ever encountered a gentleman who cares so deeply for those who depend upon him."

"Yes, he is a fine gentleman," the older woman agreed, her gaze narrowed. "But how does he make you feel?"

Amanda grimaced. "Confused. Anxious. As if I have suddenly been wakened from a long dream."

Mary abruptly chuckled, giving a sage nod of her head. "Aye. It is love."

Not finding the discomforting dilemma nearly so amusing, Amanda gave a sharp shake of her head. "How could this have happened?"

"Might as well wonder why the sun rises in the morning. It just does," Mary retorted in philosophical tones.

Amanda rolled her eyes heavenward. "Thank you, Mary. That is very helpful."

Unrepentant, the woman gave a faint shrug. "No use moaning over what cannot be changed. Now you must decide what you will do."

Amanda reluctantly accepted the truth in Mary's words.

It was futile to wish she had taken better care in guarding her heart. She could not have suspected the cold, aloof Earl of Barclay posed a danger—at least not until he had already stormed her defenses. What mattered now was how she intended to deal with her new, tenderly vulnerable emotions.

A tiny chill inched its way down her spine.

She could not deny that a small, rather cowardly part of her longed simply to give in to temptation and wed Ian. How could she not long to be close to him? To sit across the table as they enjoyed a private dinner? To awaken in his arms every morning? To bewitch him until he could not help but return her emotions?

It was that last thought that created the forbidding chill.

How many weeks, months, or even years would she be searching those handsome features for some slight indication that he cared? And how much of her heart would die if day after day she waited for naught?

After all, he had never spoken of finer emotions between them. He had never offered more than respect as his wife, and certainly never implied he wished more from her than duty to her position as Countess of Barclay.

No.

She could not bear such a fate. Far better that she walk away and attempt to put him from her thoughts. "What can I do?" she at last retorted with a faint sigh. "I cannot wed Lord Barclay."

"Even though you have given him your heart?"

"That only makes it more imperative that I find the means to free myself. I could not tolerate living with him knowing I am merely a bearable wife to him." She unconsciously squared her shoulders. "It is far better that I remain with father. At least with him I have long ago given up hope he will return my love."

Mary's face swiftly crumpled with sympathy at the unwitting edge of bitterness in her voice. "Amanda."

Angry with herself for revealing the childish pain she should have outgrown long ago, Amanda sucked in a sharp breath. "Enough of this. I have cakes to prepare."

Mary looked as if she wished to continue the conversation, but, perhaps noting the wan weariness etched onto Amanda's countenance, she gave a reluctant nod. "Very well."

Ignoring the desire to curl up in the nearest chair and sink into a blissful sleep, Amanda firmly shoved up her sleeves. There was no time for self-pity. She had a little over a month to earn the necessary money to repay her father's debt. She could not afford to waste a single moment.

Six hours later, Amanda at last pulled the last trays of cakes from the oven. Although exhausted, she had managed to regain control of her fragile composure. After helping Mary straighten the kitchen, she at last retrieved her cape and stepped into the pale November sunlight.

Stifling a yawn, she moved toward the copse of nearby trees. She had gone only a few steps, however, when the sound of Mary calling her name brought her to an abrupt halt.

Slowly turning about, she waited as Mary hurried toward her.

"Amanda, you nearly forgot this week's earnings," the older woman exclaimed, holding out a leather bag. "Over ten pounds."

Amanda accepted the bag with a faint smile. "Goodness, I had not realized we had sold so many cakes."

"We have nearly doubled our orders over the past month," Mary retorted with obvious pride. "And business is bound to be more brisk as Christmas approaches."

Amanda smothered an instinctive groan. At the moment she would happily trade her meager earnings for a decent night's sleep. Only the knowledge that every quid was precious kept her smile in place. "Who would have thought that Grandmother's jam cakes would be in such demand?"

" 'Tis your magic in creating them that makes them so special."

"Fah." Amanda gave a disbelieving shake of her head. Her only talent appeared to be staying one step ahead of disaster. "Whatever the reason, I am very close to possessing the thousand pounds I need. Soon I will be able to pay off Father's debt and be rid of my fiancé."

The proud words echoed eerily throughout the air, but they gave no comfort to Amanda's heavy heart.

She might rid herself of Lord Barclay, but she very much feared he would always possess a place in her heart.

Chapter 8

Ian stood in the shadows of the trees for what might have been an eternity.

Dark fury and undeniable pain battled within him as Amanda's words continued to burn in his mind: *I shall be rid of my fiancé.*

He had not intended to eavesdrop on the private conversation. He had simply been on his way to Worthington Hall when he had noted Amanda stepping from the cottage. It seemed like a stroke of fortune to realize he would have the opportunity to spend a few moments alone with the maiden. Since hiring the staff to fill Worthington Hall, it was increasingly difficult to discover Amanda without one servant or another about. With a decided flare of anticipation, Ian had halted beside a tree to await his future bride, not realizing he was about to discover the bitter truth.

Bloody hell.

He had suspected Amanda was far from reconciled to their upcoming wedding. There had even been moments when he feared she harbored secrets from him.

But he had never allowed himself to consider the possibility she was plotting to deceive him in such a cold, calculated fashion.

Gads, no wonder she had begged to postpone the wedding until after Christmas. He understood it all now—why she appeared so desperately weary, and why she had so anxiously hidden her hoard of coins when he entered the room.

His hands clenched into fists at his sides. Dash it all, he had eaten those jam cakes himself. At the time he had thought them delicious, not realizing they were a means to escape his wicked clutches.

His jaw tightened in an ominous manner as he thought of all he had done for Amanda.

How amused she must have been as he had struggled to please her, he seethed. She had dangled him like a fool when all along she intended to jilt him, just as Julia had done.

Only when Julia had left him at the altar, he had felt nothing but relief, a traitorous voice whispered in the back of his mind. Certainly he had not been cursed with this sharp, gnawing pain that made it nearly impossible to breathe, nor with the haunting sense of loss that clutched at his heart.

Like a wounded animal, Ian was consumed with the need to strike out. He wanted to punish Amanda for daring to treat him with such callous disregard.

And just as importantly he had to know why.

Sucking in a deep breath, he squared his shoulders and set off in the direction of Worthington Hall. He would confront Amanda with her treachery, he grimly decided. But first he intended to have a measure of revenge.

Taking little note of his surroundings, Ian followed the narrow path until he reached the manor house.

Once there, he absently greeted Forrest and, leaving his hat and coat, he went to the back parlor, where the butler assured him Amanda was enjoying tea.

Silently stepping into the room, Ian paused a moment to study the slender woman settled upon a brocade sofa. His heart flinched at the sight of her pale countenance and the droop of her proud shoulders. She looked very young and very vulnerable, he reluctantly acknowledged.

A sudden urge to pull her into his arms and comfort her was abruptly crushed as he grimly reminded himself that this woman had no desire for his comfort. In fact, she wanted nothing from him. She preferred slaving in a hot kitchen to becoming his countess.

His anger firmly restored, he strolled to the center of the room, watching as Amanda abruptly lifted her head to regard him with a startled gaze.

"My lord."

"Good afternoon, my sweet," he drawled, not missing the way her eyes darkened at his presence. "Am I in time for tea?"

With an effort, she restored her composure and reached out to tug on the velvet rope beside her. "Of course. I shall have Mrs. Hillford bring another cup."

"Thank you."

Without waiting to be asked, Ian settled himself in a nearby chair and stretched out his long legs. Perhaps sensing the tension that shimmered in the air about him, she regarded him with a hint of wariness.

"I did not expect you this morning."

"No?" Ian shrugged. "Well, I wished to speak with you concerning our engagement ball."

She stiffened at his offhand words. "Engagement ball?"

"Of course. The neighborhood will expect to celebrate our good fortune with us."

There was no mistaking the panic that rippled over her pale features. "Perhaps it would be best if we wait until after the wedding."

He slowly arched his brows, enjoying her obvious unease. "Why?"

"Well, there is very little time to plan such an event."

"My secretary already has matters in hand. You need do nothing more strenuous than consider what gown you shall wear."

"But surely . . ." Her strained words were interrupted as a middle-aged servant bustled into the room. "Oh, Mrs. Hillford, could you bring another cup and a fresh pot of tea for Lord Barclay?"

"Certainly, Miss Worthington."

"And perhaps you have some of those delicious jam cakes my cook buys from the local baker?" Ian added in smooth tones.

The housekeeper flashed him a pleased smile even as Amanda drew in a sharp, rasping breath. "Aye, sir. I shall bring them along with the tea," Mrs. Hillford promised as she turned and left the room.

Maintaining his pose of nonchalance, Ian leaned back in his chair and regarded his companion with a curious gaze. "My dear, you have gone quite pale. Are you not feeling well?"

She swallowed heavily. "I am fine."

"Surely you do not find the notion of a simple ball so terrifying?" he pressed.

"It is not that."

"Then perhaps you were offended by my request for jam cakes?" he offered.

"I do not know what you mean."

"Well, it is hardly polite to request pastries that were purchased rather than created in your own kitchen." His smile did not reach his eyes. "But they are so very delectable, are they not, my sweet?"

One trembling hand lifted to press against her bosom. A renegade, wholly unwelcome twinge of heat flared through Ian as he watched the delicate fingers against the swell of her breast, a heat he sternly dismissed with the reminder that her innocent passions had been nothing more than a deceit, like everything else about her.

"They are very good," she at last managed to croak.

His gaze deliberately narrowed. "Do you know, they remind me of the cakes that my grandmother used to make for me when I was just a lad. How much fun we would have sneaking to the kitchen to bake the cakes while the cook would wail and complain that we were destroying her kitchen. What of you, Amanda? Did your grandmother bake you jam cakes when you were just a girl?"

She gave a choked exclamation as she regarded him with dawning horror. "You know?"

Realizing his game was at an end, Ian allowed his features to harden. "You mean, do I know you are selling cakes like a common baker rather than wed me? Yes, I do."

She gave a desperate shake of her head. "How?"

Ian was not about to confess that he had been hovering in the woods, watching her like a lovesick fool. "It does not matter how I know. I desire an explanation."

Amanda's gaze briefly flickered toward the door, as if she were considering the odds of bolting before he could halt her. Then, with the courage he had once admired, she forced herself to face him squarely. "You appear to know everything."

"Not everything," he denied in dangerous tones. "I do not yet know why you would prefer to peddle cakes rather than wed me. Am I truly so repulsive?"

She appeared genuinely shocked at his question. "Of course not."

"Then why?"

Her lashes fluttered downward, intentionally shielding the expressive emerald eyes. "I told you I have no desire to wed anyone."

She was a wretched liar, he dryly acknowledged. Unlike more sophisticated women, she had yet to develop the art of allowing the untruths to drip from her lips like poisoned honey. Instead, her entire body stiffened and a hectic blush rushed to her cheeks.

"You intend to become an aging spinster at the constant demand of your father?" he demanded in disbelief.

"Eventually I hope to have a cottage of my own." She slowly lifted her gaze. "That was what I was saving for when my father became indebted to you."

A faint, unexpected stab of guilt darkened Ian's countenance. Blast it all, she was a stubborn, foolish minx. How could she not realize marriage to him could provide her with all that was lacking in her life?

"A small cottage when you could have the finest homes in England?"

Her chin tilted at his mocking words. "I do not care for fine homes or beautiful gowns or noble titles. All I desire is a home I can call my own."

Her words did nothing to ease his temper. "I am not you father. The homes I offer you will never be mortgaged or in danger of falling into ruin."

"But they will be yours, not mine," she insisted softly.

"They will be ours," he snapped. "I have told you once we are wed what is mine is yours."

The offer should have delighted her. Not every gentleman was willing to promise full control of all his possessions to a wife. More often than not, husbands kept their wives on a limited allowance that ensured they remained firmly within their power. But rather than appreciating his generosity, she was giving a sad shake of her head.

"I will still be under your control. My life will be bound to yours."

Ian surged to his feet, his eyes glittering with a silver fury. "And you believe I will prove to be a monster?" he charged in harsh tones. "Perhaps you fear I will beat you every day? Or lock you in a convenient dungeon?"

Something that might have been pain rippled over her pale countenance, and Ian briefly dared to hope she was filled with a small measure of his own torment. But within a heartbeat her expression hardened with determination.

"I do not know you well enough to foresee the future."

Suddenly Ian had endured enough. The fury that had simmered deep within him burst to the surface, and he raked his hands through his dark hair. "Bloody hell. I have done nothing but attempt to please you," he growled in frustration, longing to grasp her by the shoulders and shake some sense into her thick head. "I allowed you to put off the wedding to give you an opportunity to become more accustomed to me. I provided you a staff to ease your burdens and even desired to clothe you in a manner that befits a countess. What more could you possibly desire?"

She flinched at his sharp words, but predictably was not at all intimidated. Her hands clenched at her sides as she boldly met his glittering gaze. "I desire a husband who considers me more than a suitable countess."

Ian discovered himself caught off guard at the quiet dignity in her words. A portion of his fury faded as he regarded her with a puzzled frown. "What the devil is that supposed to mean?"

"It means you have never considered me as an actual person, with my own thoughts and needs. You have never even considered me as a wife." Her arms wrapped about her waist in an oddly vulnerable motion. "I am simply a convenient woman to fill your image of what a countess should be."

Ian opened his mouth to deny her ridiculous accusation, only to snap it closed. No, he could not reveal the truth, he acknowledged with a flare of unease. He would not confess she had fascinated him for the past three years, or that in his dreams she was no remote countess, but a passionate bride who could fulfill his deepest needs.

She had made it painfully clear she did not want to be a part of his life, even if it meant lonely destitution.

He did have his pride.

Even if it cost his very soul.

Gritting his teeth until his jaws ached, Ian offered her a rigid bow. "Very well, Miss Worthington. You wish to become a pitiful spinster with your father an eternal millstone about your neck. So be it. There are countless women eager to become my wife. Best wishes on your lonely, dreary life."

Ian turned and carefully made his way to the door.

He had to be careful.

For the first time in his life, he was blinded by tears of utter loss.

Chapter 9

The week passed in an odd haze.

Although Amanda continued with her usual routine of baking cakes and overseeing the household of Worthington Hall, she performed her duties with a sense of numb detachment. Nothing seemed capable of touching her frozen emotions—not her father's furious tirades that she was obligated to wed Lord Barclay, not the open curiosity of her neighbors, not even the overt absence of her former fiancé from Worthington Hall. It was as if her heart had been removed.

Not that she truly objected to the comforting fog, Amanda acknowledged as she sat in her drawing room with a concerned Mary. She did not doubt that all too soon the pain and loss would crash into her heart. Until then, it was a relief not to endure the ravaging emotions.

Absently adding the coins the old nurse had brought with her to the box that held her tiny savings, she heaved a faint sigh.

She was very close to the thousand pounds needed

to repay her father's debt. It was a testament to her grim determination to have achieved such a miracle. But as with everything else, Amanda felt nothing at the realization she had nearly achieved the impossible.

A heavy silence filled the room, broken only by the occasional snap of the logs burning cheerily in the fireplace. Outside gray clouds blanketed the skies, sporadically releasing a chilled drizzle. The very grayness seemed to shroud Amanda, despite the fact the room was comfortably warm.

She slowly closed the box, lifting her head to meet her old nurse's anxious gaze. She wished she possessed the words to comfort her dearest friend, but she knew nothing but time would heal her wounds.

At last the entrance of a young maid brought an end to the silence. Crossing to Amanda, she placed a folded note upon the low table near her chair before giving a curtsy and leaving the room.

Reluctantly retrieving the paper from the table, Amanda prepared herself for yet another demand from her father's tailor. Her heart nearly halted as she realized the bold, formal handwriting was not that of a local tradesman. Only one gentleman in Surrey would be sending her a missive.

Swiftly skimming through the brief message, Amanda jerkily rose to her feet. The fragile shell that had protected her heart shattered as raw pain flooded through her body.

Of all the arrogant, condescending . . . she crumpled the note into a ball and tossed it into the fire.

Understandably alarmed, Mary swiftly rose to her feet and crossed to stand beside Amanda's trembling form. "My dear, what is it?"

"Lord Barclay," she gritted.

"What did the message say?"

"That he has destroyed my father's vowels. We are to consider his debt as paid in full."

Mary regarded her in open confusion. Clearly she did not comprehend why Amanda was not overjoyed by the charitable act. "How very generous." She offered a tentative smile. "You do realize you shall be able to settle into your cottage after all?"

Amanda's expression only hardened. "No."

"Whatever do you mean?"

"The debt is one of honor," she retorted in grim tones. "It cannot simply be dismissed."

"Bah." The older woman grimaced. "It will not trouble your father."

Amanda did not doubt Mary was right. Her father would be delighted with the thought of having his debt forgotten. It would not even occur to him that by doing so he was revealing his own lack of integrity. "It will trouble me," she retorted with unswerving determination. "I will not be indebted to Lord Barclay."

Mary opened her mouth to argue. Then, noting the hectic glitter in Amanda's emerald eyes, she heaved a rueful sigh. "Ah, you have always been too stubborn for your own good."

Amanda's lips twisted as she recalled Ian's harsh words. "So I have been told."

Mary reached out to grasp her hand and pat it in a comforting manner. "Still, you must do as you see fit."

Amanda gave a slow nod of her head. Yes, there was nothing to be done but pay the debt, and as swiftly as possible. Any day Ian might return to his estate in Kent. She did not want to be brooding over their inevitable confrontation over the next several weeks, perhaps even months. Best to finish it now, she told herself sternly.

"I suppose I should not delay the inevitable," she murmured, willing her faint flare of courage to remain intact.

"What are you going to do?"

"Take what money I possess to Lord Barclay and assure him I shall have the remaining funds by Christmas." She glanced down at her fingers, which were still in Mary's hand. "I must also return his grandmother's ring."

She had not allowed herself to consider the reason she still bore Ian's ring upon her finger. Each night before going to bed, she had lectured herself on her foolishness. But even as she had determined to return the ring the following morning, she had continued to avoid performing the last symbol to end her engagement.

Now, she told herself silently, she could delay no longer.

Mary offered her a sympathetic smile as she stepped back. "Come by my cottage when you are finished with your business. We shall have a nice cup of tea."

"I will," Amanda promised, managing a weak smile as she recalled the old nurse's last attempt to comfort her with tea. "I fear I shall be in need of your special brew."

Giving Mary a swift hug, Amanda retrieved the box she had left on the table. Then, with admirable composure, she bundled herself in a heavy cloak and bonnet and set off for Meadowfield.

It took nearly half an hour to reach the estate, but while she was chilled to the bone, Amanda was relieved to discover her nerve had not failed. Allowing the butler to take her soggy outerwear, Amanda was led through the halls to the back study. A faint hint of panic struck as she lingered in the doorway, recalling their first confrontation in this room.

Once again he was seated behind his massive desk, looking impossibly handsome in his immaculately cut coat and with his dark hair brushed smoothly forward.

The perfect earl, she wryly conceded with a stab of regret. A pity he could not be plain Ian in need of a wife who could love him with all her heart.

As if sensing her scrutiny, Ian abruptly lifted his head, his silver eyes darkening with an indefinable emotion before a shuttered expression descended upon his lean features. "Miss Worthington." Tossing down his quill, Ian leaned back in his chair and regarded her with a narrowed gaze. "I feel as if we have acted out this particular performance once before."

Amanda inwardly flinched at the mocking tone, but her head remained high as she forced herself to walk toward the center of the room. "May I have a moment?"

"But of course. I always have a moment for my former fiancée." His smile was without humor. "Although I seem to have quite a collection of former fiancées these days. Please, have a seat."

"No, thank you." Amanda swallowed the lump in her throat. She had not expected Ian to make this easy for her. He did, after all, have a right to be angered by her deceit. But she had not expected the brittle bitterness she could sense in his tone. She would have thought only someone genuinely wounded could feel such bitterness. And to be wounded, he would have to have cared for her. An impossible dream. "I merely came to return your ring and give you this."

With awkward motions, she moved forward to place the box on the desk, along with the emerald ring.

A dangerous stillness cloaked his male form as Ian watched her hastily step backward. "What is it?"

"Over nine hundred pounds." She unconsciously

licked her dry lips. "I shall have the remaining money by Christmas."

With a lethal elegance, he rose to his feet, causing Amanda to take another step backward. "Did you not receive my message?"

"Yes, but I do not desire your charity, my lord."

Without warning, his hand swept the box from his desk in obvious fury. "And I do not accept money from young maidens."

She gave a startled blink at his unexpected display of emotion. "My lord, you had a bargain with my father . . ."

"A bargain you chose to break," he interrupted in harsh tones. "Tell me, my dear, when were you intending to inform me you did not intend to become my bride? Perhaps at the altar, as my previous fiancée chose to do?"

Amanda's heart clenched in pain. Gads, where was the numbing ice that had protected her this past week? "I did not come here to argue with you."

As if regretting his impulsive display, Ian raked a hand impatiently through his hair. "Good. Then take your money and be gone."

Amanda's hands clenched at her sides. Was he attempting to make this as difficult as possible? "It is your money."

"No."

"My lord."

"I said no," he burst out sharply, stepping around the desk to tower over her.

She shivered, but stubborn pride refused to allow her to be intimidated. "Are you attempting to shame me, sir?"

"Shame you?" His silver eyes darkened in angry disbelief. "What of me? You have made it clear there could be no more horrid fate than becoming my wife. Do you not believe that is shaming?"

The wound she had delivered to his pride was evident in his raw tone, and Amanda gave an unconscious shake of her head. "Becoming your wife would not be a horrid fate if you truly cared for the woman you had chosen for that position. But no maiden wishes to be a mere decoration."

His lips thinned as he abruptly spun on his heel and paced across the room. Reaching the fireplace, he leaned an arm upon the mantel and gazed into the smoldering embers. "You believe I do not care?"

His words were so low that for a moment Amanda was uncertain if she heard him correctly. Then she glared at his rigidly held back. "You won me in a card game, my lord," she said in tones that could not completely hide her searing pain. How dare he make a mockery of what she so desperately desired? "Besides, you made it painfully clear during our first interview your only interest was in a woman who would become your countess without complaint and not be a thorough embarrassment."

Her words seemed to echo through the room as Ian continued to stare into the fireplace. Then, with a harsh breath, he turned to face her with a startlingly vulnerable expression. "I said a great number of foolish things during our first interview. I somehow thought I would only frighten you more if I were honest with you."

Caught off guard, Amanda gazed at him with wary confusion. "What do you mean?"

"I did not want you as my wife because you were convenient," he ground out. "Good gads, I cannot conceive of a more inconvenient woman than you. I wanted you

because I could not get you out of my thoughts. You
had become my obsession."

Amanda sucked in a sharp breath. "Me?"

"Yes, you." He returned to stand before her, his gaze
running a restless path over her disbelieving expression. "I would watch you from afar, admiring your courage and dignity. I did everything in my power to become
better acquainted, but you were so vexingly elusive.
When your father offered me your hand, it seemed like
a heaven-sent opportunity."

"But you were so indifferent," she charged, her emotions too battered to be easily exposed to further disappointment. "You made me believe any woman would
do."

The handsome features grimaced with regret at her
accusation. "As I said, I, perhaps ridiculously, presumed
you would be more comfortable with the notion that
ours would be an arrangement of convenience. And I
suppose I was also hoping to convince myself that was
the reason I had so swiftly accepted your father's offer.
It was easier than admitting I had to have you no matter
how despicable my methods."

Amanda searched his countenance, seeking some
cruel jest meant to punish her further. But there was
nothing to be found beyond a tender uncertainty that
wrenched her heart. "You truly wanted me?" she whispered.

His silver eyes darkened to smoke as he reached out
to gently cup her cheek. "You cannot believe a gentleman who would devote every waking moment to
thoughts of how he can best please a maiden could be
indifferent. That is not even to mention the endless
nights I have paced the floor recalling the sweetness of
your kisses."

A tentative, decidedly precarious flame of hope flickered to life deep in her heart. Still, she needed to hear the truth from his own lips. "Are you trying to say you care for me?"

He gave a rueful chuckle. "Egads, I would think it was embarrassingly obvious."

Amanda abruptly reached up to grasp the lapels of his coat, the faint flame shimmering to radiant joy. He did care. "Not to a thick-skulled maiden who was too stubborn to realize she possessed the finest, most generous gentleman in all of England."

His hand shifted to grasp her chin, his fingers trembling as he desperately gazed deeply into her wide eyes. "What did you say?"

Amanda deliberately pressed herself against his hard form, breathing in his warm male heat. "I think I said I love you, Lord Barclay."

"Amanda." With a harsh groan, his head swooped downward to capture a swift, utterly bewitching kiss. Slowly lifting his head, he regarded her with eyes that blazed with happiness. "Dear lord, I thought I had lost you. I was a fool to accept your father's bargain."

Her hand rose to boldly trace the lips that caused such delicious flutters deep within her. "You mean I am not worth a thousand pounds?" she teased.

His arms encircled her waist to mold her even more closely to his body. "You are more precious than any gold or any jewel," he promised in low tones, brushing his lips over her forehead. Then, without warning, he dropped onto one knee and tilted his head back to meet her startled gaze. "On this occasion I will do it right. Miss Worthington, will you do me the very great honor of becoming my wife? I promise to care for you, to cherish you, and to love you with every breath that I take."

Giddy, breathtaking joy rushed through Amanda. Barely aware of what she was doing, she sank to her knees and threw her arms about his neck.

"Yes. Yes, I will marry you."

"After Christmas?" he growled, cupping her face in his hands.

"Today. Tomorrow. Whenever you desire."

"I believe I have been a good enough lad for an early Christmas present."

"Oh yes," she agreed, her fingers plunging into the ebony satin of his hair. "A very, very good lad."

Chapter 10

The yuletide ball was as perfect as Ian had dreamed it would be.

No, it was even better than he dreamed, he acknowledged, pulling his lovely wife closer to his side. Watching the elegant guests twirl across the dance floor, he was filled with a deep contentment.

Certainly Amanda had proven to be just as worthy a countess as he had hoped. In the past fortnight, she had won the hearts of his staff and tenants with her genuine concern and relentless devotion to ensure they were given the proper care. And she was certainly as gloriously beautiful as he suspected in her new emerald gown, which revealed a bewitching amount of alabaster skin.

But his contentment did not come from her skills as Countess of Barclay. Instead, the unwavering love that shimmered in her eyes and her ready passion had kept him lingering in his bed with indecent frequency.

Smiling with what he suspected was hopeless devotion, he glanced down at his bride. "Well, my dear, I believe you may consider your first ball a resounding success."

She gave a pleased chuckle at his compliment. "If it is, then it is entirely due to your secretary's efforts. He possesses an uncanny talent for overseeing the most mundane details. Do you know he personally arranged the holly to ensure it was done correctly?"

His hand covertly moved to stroke the bare skin at the back of her neck. "Do not underestimate yourself, my sweet. You possess your own uncanny talents. Talents I deeply appreciate."

Amanda's ready blush added a delightful color to her cheeks, but Ian did not miss the revealing shiver that raced through her body. "My lord."

His own blood began to heat with delicious anticipation and, grasping her hand, he placed it firmly upon his arm. With a casual disregard he was far from feeling, he began to slowly steer them through the crowded doorway. "Indeed, I cannot wait to experience a small sampling of that talent."

Her eyes widened in shock. "Ian, we cannot leave our guests."

"We will be gone but a moment," he assured her, leading her toward a distant room he had prepared earlier in the day.

"Really, sir, you are incorrigible," she protested, but she made no effort to free herself as they continued down the hall.

"I do try." He waggled his brows in a wicked fashion.

She stifled her instinctive laugh. "Where are we going?"

"Does it matter?"

She came to an abrupt halt, gazing at him with enough love to melt the recently fallen snow. "No. Not as long as we are together."

His heart lurched as he swooped down to claim a sweet, lingering kiss. "We shall be together an eternity, Lady Barclay," he promised in husky tones.

Her emerald eyes darkened. "That should be just enough time to prove how much I love you."

Just for a moment, the muted sounds of music and laughter receded, leaving Ian alone with his lovely bride. He silently allowed his heart to swell with love before giving a rueful shake of his head. "Gads, you bewitch me. But I will not be distracted. I have a surprise for you."

"Another surprise?" she demanded, her fingers lifting to touch the exquisite ruby necklace he had presented to her just before the ball.

"I did promise to be a most indulgent husband," he reminded her, firmly moving to the door at the end of the hall.

She smiled with obvious contentment. "So you did."

"Close your eyes," he commanded, waiting for her to obediently lower her lids before opening the door and leading her to the center of the room. "All right, now you may open them."

She slowly lifted her heavy lashes and glanced about the barren room with obvious curiosity.

"What is it?"

"Look up."

Tilting back her head, she at last noted the endless bundles of mistletoe Ian had ordered to be hung across the open-beamed ceiling.

"Dear heavens," she breathed in disbelief. "Wherever did you acquire so much mistletoe?"

"My ever capable secretary."

She lowered her gaze to regard him with a smoldering pleasure. "What a very clever gentleman he is."

"Indubitably," he readily agreed, slipping his arms

about her waist to draw her close. "Now, my dear countess, I believe we have a considerable task ahead of us if we are to kiss beneath all these mistletoes before we are missed."

She readily slid her hands about his neck as her eyes glowed with happiness. "Do not concern yourself, my lord," she murmured. "Although a perfect countess might avoid causing a scandal at her own ball, a loving wife doesn't give a fig for gossip. She would much rather spend her evening in the arms of her handsome husband."

Ian gave a low groan of satisfaction, his head lowering toward the temptation of her rose petal lips. "Thank goodness I did not choose a perfect countess."

LITTLE JAM CAKES

1 C. sugar
4 eggs, separated
1 tsp. vanilla
1 T. lemon juice
Pinch of salt
1 ½ C. flour (measured, then sifted)
1 C. butter (melted)
1 C. favorite jam

Beat egg yolks until thick and add in the sugar, vanilla, and lemon juice. Fold in sifted flour and salt alternately with melted butter. When thoroughly smooth, fold in egg whites that have been beaten stiffly. Line muffin pans with paper cups. Place a spoonful of batter in the bottom of each cup and add a spoonful of jam. Cover with remaining batter. Bake for 15 to 25 minutes (depending on size) in a 350 degree (F) oven.

MINCE PIE AND MISTLETOE

Joy Reed

Chapter 1

It lay in the gutter, half hidden by a pile of fallen leaves. Ellie spied it as she was coming out of the milliner's shop, buttoning her pelisse against the December cold. It was sheerest luck that she did, for her mind was on other things. She had just seen a most elegant new shawl in Miss Asher's shop, and it broke her heart to think she could not buy it.

"A very handsome article, ain't it, miss? And quite indistinguishable from a real India one," Miss Asher had said as Ellie wistfully fingered the shawl's rich red and gold fringe. Ellie was sure it would have looked lovely with her new white dress. But the price of the shawl was fixed at a guinea, and that put it out of reach as far as Ellie was concerned. A guinea might be cheap for a shawl that was indistinguishable from a real India one, but it was a great deal for a girl whose pin money was as limited as hers.

In any case, the greater part of her allowance for the quarter had been spent for the satin and net and other materials that had gone into making up her new evening dress. And of course she had needed a new dress much more than a new shawl. She could hardly wear an old dress to the Winwoods' party.

The Winwoods' annual ball on December twenty-seventh was always one of the chief events of the Christmas season in the village, and this year's ball was even more important than usual. It was common knowledge that at some point during the evening, the engagement between Gregory Winwood and Cecelia Lake would be announced.

This in itself was not so important, for it had been an understood thing for some months that Gregory and Cecelia would make a match of it. But there had been certain passages between Gregory and Ellie in the past that made Ellie determined to look unusually well that evening, lest anyone be tempted to suppose she was not perfectly happy to see him marry Cecelia.

It was not that Ellie had ever been in love with Gregory. He was a nice boy, and she had been glad enough to receive his attentions as long as he was inclined to bestow them, but when he had transferred them to Cecelia she had accepted his defection philosophically. Still, she would have been more than human if she had not felt some lingering sense of pique. It was not pleasant to think she had been spurned for Cecelia Lake, who was a silly goose if there ever was one, even if she did have jet black hair and big dark eyes. Ellie did not have jet black hair and big dark eyes. She had fair hair and blue eyes, and she reckoned it was only a matter of taste that made the one more desirable than the other. She was resolved to show Gregory and everyone else how lamentable had been his taste in preferring Cecelia to herself.

The shawl would have been a help in this. It was just such a one as Ellie had seen depicted in the latest fashion paper, worn by a simpering miss with clustered dark curls and unnaturally large dark eyes, who looked very much like Cecelia herself. Ellie had no guinea to spare, however, and so she had been forced to leave the shawl behind in the milliner's shop. But as she came wistfully forth, buttoning her pelisse against the cold, her eyes caught a glimmer of gold in the gutter.

It can't be anything, Ellie told herself. *Only a bit of rubbish. A scrap of paper, perhaps, or an empty sweet tin.* Still, she had enough curiosity to walk over and inspect the object more closely. The gleam of gold was unmistakable now amid the sodden mass of leaves and litter in the gutter. Cautiously Ellie prodded aside the leaves with the toe of her boot. And there it lay in all its glory—a golden guinea, glinting up at her like the visible answer to a prayer.

With an exclamation, Ellie picked it up. She turned it over in her hand, marveling to find such a thing in the village street. *How could it have gotten here?* she wondered. *Someone must have dropped it.* She looked up and down the street, but there was no one to be seen.

It was Christmas Eve, the hour was late, and most people were already in their homes preparing for the coming holiday. It was merest chance that she, Ellie, still happened to be abroad.

Her mother had needed a few extra lemons for the mince pies she was making, and Ellie had volunteered to run out and get them before the shops closed. Having bought the lemons at the grocer's, she had then succumbed to the temptation to look in Miss Asher's shop, which was still open along with a few others along the street. And it was a fortunate thing that she had. Here she had found a guinea, the very amount she had been wishing for only a moment before. She might go and buy her shawl this minute if she wished—the red and gold one that would look so handsome with her new white dress.

Still, Ellie hesitated, turning the guinea over in her hand. She felt guilty at the thought of spending it, almost as though she were stealing from someone. But this was not at all the case, as her conscience assured her. The guinea must have been lying in the gutter for some time, or it would not have been covered with leaves—leaves that had fallen more than a month ago. Obviously its owner had not been searching for it very energetically. Likely he had given it up for lost the moment he discovered it was gone—not surprisingly, perhaps, for few people would be honest enough to return such a prize if they were lucky enough to find it in the first place.

Of course she, Ellie, would have returned the guinea if that were possible, but she really had no clue from whence it had come. It was a perfectly anonymous guinea with no mark of ownership about it, and it might have fallen directly from heaven, for all Ellie knew to the contrary.

And indeed, it seems almost as though it must have, Ellie told herself with a smile. *What a piece of luck! I'll go buy the shawl this instant, before Miss Asher closes for the night.*

Just as she reached the shop door, she encountered an elderly woman coming down the sidewalk with slow, shuffling steps. There was a market basket slung over her arm and a shawl thrown over her grizzled head. "Good evening, Mrs. Beale," said Ellie, smiling at the woman. "You're late abroad this Christmas Eve!"

"Ah, it's Miss Roswell," said Mrs. Beale, her wrinkled face lighting up with a smile. "And so are you late abroad, my dear. What brings you out this time o' night?"

Ellie explained about the mince pies.

"Ah, I've had the privilege of tasting your mother's

mince pies," said Mrs. Beale, with a nod. "Delicious they are. I've often said there's nobody in the village whose mince pies can compare to Mrs. Roswell's. But there, I mustn't be keeping you. If she sent you after lemons, you'd best be getting along home with them so she can finish her baking."

"Yes, and you will be wanting to get home, too, I'm sure," said Ellie. "It's growing late." Smiling, she indicated the market basket. "I take it you've been buying your Christmas dinner?"

"Oh, aye," said Mrs. Beale with a half-suppressed sigh. "That I have. You know my son Arthur's home from the war, of course."

Ellie nodded. It was common knowledge that Arthur Beale had returned from the Peninsular War with a wounded leg. "You must be so pleased to have him home," she said. "It seems a great many years since he went away. I can't even remember how many it is now. Has it been five or six?"

"Six," said Mrs. Beale, with another half-suppressed sigh. "And I must say it'll be wonderful to sit down to Christmas dinner with him again. Only I wish I could be giving him a goose for his dinner, as we used to have in the old days when his father was alive. It's foolish of me, no doubt, but Christmas doesn't seem like Christmas without a roasted goose on the table. I'd hoped I might be able to manage it, but what with one thing and another I find it isn't possible. Geese are so dear this year, you know, and we just got done paying the bill for the doctor for Arthur's leg. The upshot is, I find I'll have to make do with a bit of beef instead of a goose for Christmas dinner."

"That's too bad," said Ellie sympathetically. "Beef is all very well, of course, but naturally you would rather have a goose for such a special occasion."

Mrs. Beale agreed that she would, but added more cheerfully, "Still, I doubt Arthur will make any complaint about it. He tells me they had to eat horseflesh once or twice when they was over in Spain. Compared to horseflesh, honest British beef ought to taste as good as any goose ever roasted!"

Ellie laughed and agreed that it ought to. "Well, Merry Christmas, Mrs. Beale," she said. "And tell Arthur Merry Christmas, too."

Mrs. Beale said that she would, and wished Ellie a Merry Christmas in return. She then set off down the street again with her market basket. Ellie did not immediately enter the milliner's shop, but stood watching the elderly woman as she shuffled down the sidewalk, her head bent and her shoulders bowed. Something in her stooping figure stirred Ellie to a sense of guilt.

She cannot even afford a goose for Christmas dinner, Ellie told herself. *She must make do with beef instead for herself and her wounded son. And here I am about to buy a shawl I don't really need, only so I can queen it at the Winwoods' party.*

Again Ellie looked down at the guinea in her hand. It seemed to wink up at her, full of irresistible promise and unlimited possibility. Ellie looked at it a moment longer, then turned with sudden resolution and made her way past the milliner's shop, back toward the grocer's on the next block.

Mr. Snodgrass greeted her with pleasure but some surprise. "What, back again, Miss Roswell?" he exclaimed. "I didn't look to see you again so soon. Don't tell me you need more lemons?"

"No, no lemons. In fact, I don't need anything for

myself at all, Mr. Snodgrass. I wanted to buy something for someone else instead—a Christmas gift, if you will." With many a blush and stammer, Ellie explained that she wished to buy a goose and have it sent to the Beales. "Could I do that?" she asked anxiously. "I have this guinea to pay for it." She laid the guinea on the counter.

Mr. Snodgrass picked up the guinea and regarded it with speculation and a touch of awe. "Oh, aye, that ought to buy you the finest goose that ever walked on two legs," he said. "Of course, properly speaking I don't sell geese. That's my brother Tom's business, you know, and he's already shut up for the night." He nodded toward the adjoining butcher's shop, now dark and shuttered. "But seeing as Tom and I are in the way of being partners, I don't think that need be any bar to sending out your goose tonight. I'll have my Will run next door to pick one up, and I'll make all right with Tom in the morning when he comes in."

Ellie thanked him profusely, but Mr. Snodgrass waved aside her thanks with a magnanimous air. "Oh, you needn't thank me, Miss Roswell. It's a pleasure to be able to lend a hand in such a good deed. It's a very nice thing you're doing—a very nice thing indeed. I'm sure the Beales will be very grateful to you."

The idea of the Beales' gratitude was a pleasant one to Ellie, yet somehow it struck a wrong chord. She frowned. A memory was teasing at her thoughts—the memory of a sermon the vicar had preached a few weeks ago. He had taken for his text, "But when thou doest alms, let not thy left hand know what thy right hand doeth," and had gone on to make a convincing case for doing one's acts of charity anonymously. "Let us not be like the hypocrites who sound a trumpet when they do their good deeds, seeking the glory of men," he had told the congregation solemnly. "Let us remember rather that virtue is its own reward."

Ellie had been most impressed with these words at the time. As they recurred to her now, she found her resolution was suddenly taken. "Oh, but I don't want the Beales to know anything about my sending the goose," she told Mr. Snodgrass in a rush. "I want it to be a secret. Merely tell them it is from an anonymous benefactor who wishes them well."

Mr. Snodgrass looked surprised by this, but readily agreed to keep Ellie's good deed a secret. Repeating that it was a very nice thing she was doing, he wished her a merry Christmas and bowed her out of the shop as impressively as though she had been a queen.

As Ellie walked home through the cold December twilight, she was conscious of a glowing sense of satisfaction. The Beales would have their goose now, and it was delightful to imagine Mrs. Beale's surprise and pleasure when the grocer's boy delivered it.

Yet there was an undercurrent of wistfulness in Ellie's thoughts. The shawl was lost forever to her now. It was not to be imagined that an article of such elegance could remain unsold for long. By the time she had received her next quarter's allowance, it would undoubtedly be adorning the back of some luckier girl.

Well, never mind, Ellie told herself firmly. *I would have always felt guilty if I had spent that money selfishly on myself. This way, the Beales will have their goose, and I can rest content knowing I am helping them to have a merry Christmas.* With which sustaining thought, she hastened her steps toward home.

Chapter 2

After bidding Ellie good evening, Mr. Snodgrass returned to his place behind the counter. "That's a nice girl, Will," he told his assistant as he put her guinea in the cashbox. "A very nice girl indeed. It's not many girls who would have thought of doing such a thing."

Will gave an affirmative grunt. He was busy arranging some bags of chestnuts at the end of the counter, stacking them into a neat pyramid. Mr. Snodgrass, watching him, was conscious of an idea stirring in his head. Ellie's generous gesture had impressed him very much. The Roswells were a nice, genteel family, but everybody knew they were far from wealthy. He, Augustus Snodgrass, was likewise far from wealthy, but his business was a thriving concern, as the day's receipts would certainly bear out. With Ellie's guinea added in, they ought to total a most satisfactory sum. Of course, the guinea was really his brother Tom's and would eventually have to be accounted as such, but even without it he could afford to make a generous gesture if he liked.

With sudden resolution, he turned to his assistant.

"Let's put the shutters up now, Will," he said. "It's getting late, and we're not likely to see much more trade tonight. Besides, you've still got to take that goose round to the Beales."

"Aye," agreed Will. As he moved toward the door, Mr. Snodgrass added casually, "Oh, and Will, as long as you're going to the Beales', take 'em one of those bags of chestnuts. And take one home for your mother as well," he added in an unpremeditated burst of generosity. It was Christmas Eve, after all, and Christmas came but once a year, as he reminded himself. Will was a good worker and deserved a bonus even in addition to his day's holiday.

"Aye," said Will again. He spoke as laconically as before, but inwardly he was surprised. Mr. Snodgrass was a fair man, as he was willing to admit when under the mellowing influence of a pint of beer, but never before had he given Will so much as a groat beyond his wages. Now he was giving him a whole bag of chestnuts.

The gesture gained an additional weight through being so unexpected, and Will felt a warm sense of gratification as he went out to put up the shutters. Clearly his stock was running high with old Snodgrass. His mother would be pleased—pleased by the gift, but more pleased by this palpable evidence of his employer's approbation.

It was her constant fear that Will would lose his position through some trifling lapse of attention—the time he had come in late after a more than usually convivial night at the Bull, for instance. But now he could show her that his position was, on the contrary, quite secure. Old Snodgrass would hardly be giving out chestnuts to an employee he was planning to dismiss!

The thought pleased Will so much that he began to whistle an off-key rendition of *God Rest Ye Merry Gentle-*

men as he went about his work of putting up the shutters. Snow crunched on the ground under his feet, and the air was full of swirling white flakes. Will, glancing up at the sky, thought it looked as though a regular storm was under way and reflected philosophically that it was quite seasonal weather for Christmas.

As he came around the corner of the shop, he nearly collided with a dark-haired gentleman who was standing there on the sidewalk. The gentleman was a stranger to Will and dressed in a manner that even Will's provincial eyes recognized as being the height of fashion. He was looking after a lady who was just vanishing around the corner. Will, squinting against the snow, identified the lady as Miss Roswell, who had been in the shop but a moment before.

Having watched until Ellie was out of sight, the stranger turned around and for the first time encountered Will's interested scrutiny. "Good evening," he said in a pleasant deep voice. "I wonder if you might be able to assist me? I'm a stranger to these parts and in need of lodging for the night. Do you happen to know of an inn somewhere hereabouts?"

It was quite unnecessary for him to say he was a stranger. Will was acquainted with every person in the immediate neighborhood, and he knew well he had never laid eyes on this gentleman before. That he was a gentleman Will could not doubt, but he had in full measure the provincial's typical distrust toward "foreigners," and if it had been an ordinary day he would probably have directed the strange gentleman on to the next village and counted him good riddance. But Will was still feeling elated about his bonus, and this, together with the stranger's pleasant manner, made him set aside his prejudices for the moment. "Aye, the Bull's just around the corner there," he said, nodding in the direction indicated. "It's a tidy place, and Mrs. Merriweather will be able to put you up, I don't doubt."

The stranger thanked him and bestowed a coin upon him by way of a tip, a generous gesture that further mitigated Will's prejudices. *A very pleasant-spoken, open handed gentleman,* he told himself as he put up the shutters. *We could use a few more such around here.*

Then he dismissed the incident from his mind to dwell pleasurably once more upon his mother's probable reaction when he brought home the chestnuts.

As Will had expected, Mrs. Dennis was delighted by Mr. Snodgrass's gift. "Why, that was right nice of him, Will," she said, happily surveying the bag of chestnuts. "A very nice gesture, upon my word. You know I've always been fond of chestnuts. And his giving them to you this way—well, it seems to show he thinks a great deal of you, doesn't it? I'm gladder than I can say to see you making good."

Will said modestly that he didn't suppose the chestnuts meant much and that it was only Old Snodgrass's way of showing holiday spirit. "But I knew you'd be glad to have them, Ma," he added. "Being as you're so fond of them and all. They'll make a nice treat for us after dinner tomorrow."

"Aye, that they will. Why, it'll be a rare feast we'll be having, with the goose and the pudding and chestnuts and all. I wonder now . . . I wonder. . . ." Mrs. Dennis's face took on a pensive look.

"Yes, Ma?" encouraged her son.

Mrs. Dennis looked down at her work-worn hands. "I wonder if I shouldn't be asking your Uncle Robert to dinner tomorrow," she said softly. "Of course we've been at outs these many years—that old quarrel that I've told you of so many times. I always swore I wouldn't speak the first word, seeing as it was him who started the trouble. He *would* keep talking so bitter against your father—"

Will nodded. He had heard many times how his Uncle Robert had opposed his sister's marrying the late William Dennis.

His mother went on, still looking down at her hands. "In the general way, I pride myself on keeping my word," she said. "And I'd keep it now if I could see any virtue in it. But I'm starting to wonder if perhaps I've let pride blind me to doing my Christian duty. Your father's been gone these five years now, and he was never a man to hold a grudge himself, bless his heart. He'd be the first to say let bygones be bygones. Now we've got all these lovely chestnuts, and food enough to feed half a dozen folk besides ourselves, and with its being Christmas and all—well, it does seem a shame to keep up an old quarrel any longer. As I say, I'm tempted to send a message to Robert saying I'm willing to forget the past if he is. We're none of us getting any younger, and I can't help thinking how dreadful I'd feel if something was to happen that I wouldn't get a chance to talk to Robert again. What I mean is, if I had to live out the rest of my life knowing I could have done something about mending our quarrel and didn't, to say I'd feel bad wouldn't half express it."

There was a quaver in her voice as she spoke these last words and a glitter in her eyes that looked suspiciously like tears. Will could see how greatly she longed to be reunited with the brother from whom she had been estranged for twenty-five years.

Accordingly, he put aside his own reservations and encouraged her to sit down and write a note of invitation to his uncle. Then, although the snow was falling more heavily than ever, he put on his boots and overcoat and walked the two miles that lay between his mother's cottage and Wyngate, the country estate where his uncle was employed as caretaker.

Robert Fowler was surprised to receive a visit from his nephew. Thanks to his long-standing quarrel with his sister, he had only a nodding acquaintance with Will and had never exchanged more than a word or two with him when they happened to meet publicly in the village. But his surprise at Will's unexpected visit was as nothing when he learned the reason for it.

"Ma said she'd be very happy if you could see your way clear to coming," Will explained as Robert read slowly and painstakingly through his sister's note. "Of course, you may already have plans of your own, in which case she'd understand if you couldn't come. But if you can, she'd be very glad to see you. On account of its being Christmas and all. . . ."

"Aye," agreed Robert. He was struggling to hide his pleasure behind his usual dour demeanor. "Christmas dinner, you say? Well, well, a bite and sup at the Bull was as far as my plans for the day went, but I don't suppose Mrs. Merriweather would feel it if I were to stay away. It's not as though I'm expected, after all. Since your mother asks it . . . aye, you can tell her I'll come. Tomorrow early, you say? Aye, I'll be there soon as I can finish up my duties here."

After Will had gone, Robert took up the note and painstakingly spelled through it once more. He was not an accomplished reader by any means, but the letter was written so clearly even he could make no mistake. Amy was begging him to set aside their quarrel and be friends again after all these years.

Robert was deeply touched by her letter. Although he had tried for twenty-five years to justify his behavior at the time of his sister's marriage, he had known almost from the start he had been wrong. He had had no business to say the things he had said to Amy. True, Amy had said some harsh things, too, but only after he had called the man she loved shiftless and of no account. Feeling as she did about William Dennis, it was not unnatural she should resent such accusations.

And in fact, his accusations had proven groundless. William Dennis had made Amy an admirable husband. The two of them had lived together happily until William's death a few years before. Yet in a way, that had only made Robert's situation worse. If his sister had been unhappy in her marriage, then he would have felt he could have afforded to be generous. It would have been a point of pride with him to extend her all the aid and comfort that he, as her brother, could provide. But as it was, he had been wrong from start to finish. That being the case, he either had to admit he was wrong or sever all connection between himself and his sister's family.

He had chosen to follow the latter course. It had seemed the preferable alternative to eating humble pie in such undiluted quantity. Yet as the years had passed and the breach had widened between him and his nearest kin, he had begun to suspect that in salvaging his pride he had lost something much more valuable. He had always been fond of Amy, and she of him. They had had good times together as children, and later, after their parents had died, they had been all in all to each other. Now they were less to each other than strangers.

There had been times in the last twenty-five years when Robert had longed to admit his mistake and ask Amy for forgiveness. But he had never dared to act on this longing. He reasoned that, having compounded his original error through so many years of pigheaded silence, Amy would want nothing to do with him. Likely she would shut the door in his face if he ever dared call on her and attempt to beg her pardon. So he had gone on from year to year, withdrawing more and more from the life of the village, a lonely, embittered old man whose bitterness was directed at nobody so much as himself.

And now, out of the blue, Amy had written to invite him to Christmas dinner. It quite turned him head over heels to think of it. As he read through the letter once again, spelling out the words with painstaking deliberation, the thing that struck Robert most strongly was the fact that Amy never once referred to his own part in the quarrel. She merely begged him to set aside their differences and be friends once again. Differences! Such differences as there had been were all his doing, as she very well knew. Yet not only had she been willing to take equal share in the blame, she had been the first to extend a hand in reconciliation.

The thought made Robert's heart swell with a mixture of love and remorse. *That's just like Amy,* he told himself. *She was always a generous little thing . . . as generous a soul as ever drew breath, 'pon my word.*

He made up his mind that he would be generous, too, this once. He would appear at his sister's cottage early tomorrow in the most festive garments he could muster. It went to his heart that he had nothing more festive in his wardrobe than the old black coat and well-worn boots he had been wearing these fifteen years.

It also went to his heart that he could not muster anything in the nature of a Christmas gift for Amy. He had always managed to scrape up some kind of a gift for her in the old days, no matter how hard-pressed his financial state. Then he recollected that Wyngate's wine cellar was still largely intact, and as caretaker he had full access to such booty as it might contain. In the normal way, Will was conscientious to a fault, and he would have considered it as much stealing to take a bottle of wine from the house as any other of its furnishings, but for an occasion of such moment he felt he might suspend his normal scruples.

Besides, he reasoned, it would be easy enough to stop by the Bull on the way home and buy another bottle to replace the one he took.

So he got out his keys and made a trip into the cellars, selecting a particularly dusty, cobwebby bottle of port that seemed to promise well. Then he brushed up his coat, polished his old boots, and went to bed, feeling more excited than he had felt for many a Christmas.

When he was actually on the way to Amy's cottage the next day, however, with a sprig of laurel in his hatband and the bottle of port tucked beneath his arm, he found himself prey to a sudden nervousness. Ever since the letter had arrived, he had been so busy dwelling on how delightful it would be to be reunited with Amy that he had given no thought to the reunion itself. Now he was suddenly struck by how awkward it was likely to prove.

What would he say to Amy? And what would she say to him? She had abstained from making him any reproach in her letter, but it was possible she might not be so forbearing in person. Likely there would be reproaches of some kind to endure. Robert's face hardened. He was half minded to return to Wyngate and avoid any risk of such an event.

Then he remembered that the blame for the past lay

wholly with him, and that even if it had not, Amy had been the first to extend an olive branch in reconciliation. Such a generous and courageous act ought to earn her the right to say what she pleased. So he continued on his way, but his steps were slower than before, and when he finally reached the cottage where Amy and her son lived, it took all his courage to knock upon the holly-festooned door.

The door was opened instantly by Amy herself. She was a middle-aged woman now, rather stout about the middle and rather graying as to hair, but her eyes were as clear and blue as ever and her smile as sweet. As Robert looked at her, the years seemed to fall away, and he saw only the little Amy he had thought lost forever. "Amy," he said, holding out his arms in wordless supplication. "Amy!"

"Robert," she said with a half-choked cry, and fell into his arms. She was laughing and crying at the same time, and Robert found there was a suspicious moisture in his own eyes as he held her tightly against him. "Oh, Robert," she wept. "I've been such a fool not to write to you sooner. I should have said something, years ago, and put an end to this dreadful, foolish business—"

"Nonsense," said Robert, patting her shoulder. "Nonsense! It was I who was wrong, Amy, not you. If I hadn't been a fool, I'd have admitted it sooner and saved all this trouble. So many years—so many wasted years—" His voice failed him, so that all he could do was tighten his hold on his sister with wordless emotion.

The two siblings' mutual self-reproaches might have continued for some time had not Will that moment appeared in the doorway behind his mother. His expression was reserved, but a keen observer might have detected approval in his eyes as he stood watching her weep in Robert's arms. Mrs. Dennis, becoming aware of him, stopped crying long enough to introduce him to her brother. "But I know him," protested Will. "I've seen him in the village any time these twenty years—"

"Yes, but not to speak to," said Mrs. Dennis firmly. "And not as your uncle, Will. This is your Uncle Robert, and I hope you and he'll be friends now that we've put this foolish quarrel of ours behind us."

With a diffident air, Robert extended his hand to his nephew. Will took it and shook it, with an air fully as diffident as his own. This formality concluded, Mrs. Dennis insisted they all go into the house and sit down.

"Take your uncle to the parlor now, Will, while I go see to the dinner," she instructed her son. "May the good Lord have mercy! I've been that busy talking, it'll be a wonder if the goose isn't burnt to a crisp and the pudding boiled dry."

Mercifully, neither of these dreadful possibilities had come to pass. The goose, when Mrs. Dennis finally brought it to the table, proved to be done to a turn, while Robert declared the pudding a masterpiece of the pastrymaker's art. Indeed, it seemed to him he had never eaten a better dinner.

He said as much several times, causing Amy to beam and say she was glad he hadn't lost his taste for her cooking. They chatted and reminisced about old times, Will taking little part in the conversation but listening with interest to all that was said.

When they had all eaten as much dinner as they could hold, they opened Robert's port, put a shovelful of chestnuts on the fire, and retired to the fireside to talk some more.

Under the genial influence of a glass or two of port, Will became more talkative. Robert was able to draw out of him some account of his present concerns as well as his hopes for the future. He found himself quite pleased with the character of his nephew. Will seemed a likely young man, hard-working and enterprising and none the worse for being a trifle closemouthed. Robert had the reputation of being closemouthed himself.

He began to turn in his head the notion of doing something for his nephew in the coming years. He had always been of a saving disposition, and there was a goodly sum laid up in his name at the banker's. Why should he not leave it to his nephew when he himself had no further need of it?

But all that could be left to the future, as Robert reflected comfortably, leaning back in his chair and taking another sip of port. For now it was enough to bask in the warmth of the fire and the company of his family—*his* family, with whom he was once more on amicable terms. ·

It was late when he reluctantly wrenched himself away from family and fireside and made ready to return to Wyngate. Mrs. Dennis was of the opinion he ought not to return there at all that night. She said it was uncommon cold outside, that she and Will could very well put him up for the night, and that she did not like to think of him walking all that way to Wyngate by himself in the dark.

But Robert had ever been conscientious in matters relating to his employment, and he did not feel it right to absent himself from his duties any longer. So he bade his sister and nephew good night, promised to call again soon, and set out to make his way over the fields to Wyngate.

His sister had not erred in calling it a cold night. Robert scarcely felt its chill, however, for his heart had been so thoroughly warmed by the fires of familial love and fellowship that his body was warmed right along with it. Still, when he reached the Bull, he decided it would not hurt to stop and drink a pint of beer before continuing on his way to Wyngate.

In truth, it was the lure of companionship as much as fire and home brew that drew him. The sound of voices and laughter issuing from the taproom sounded very attractive to his ears. He had never been a social man, and in recent years had indeed been something of a hermit in his habits, but tonight his heart was overflowing with good feeling toward everyone and everything—a sort of living embodiment of the sentiment, "Peace on earth, goodwill toward men."

Besides, Robert rationalized, *if I stop at the Bull, I can buy a bottle of port to replace the one I gave to Amy. It's as well I should do it tonight, for I hadn't really any right to take the other, and my conscience won't be easy until I replace it.*

Having thus reconciled duty and pleasure, he turned his steps toward the Bull, where the sound of laughter seemed to beckon him with the promise of pleasant companionship.

Chapter 3

For the past several weeks, Christopher Garret had felt like a stranger in a strange land.

Although an Englishman born, it had been eleven years since he had set foot on English soil. He had gone out to India as a young man of twenty-two to make his fortune, like so many other young men possessed of more industry and initiative than ready cash. And in fact he *had* made his fortune—a modest fortune compared to some, but of sufficient size to enable him to return to England and live in decent comfort without the necessity of taking a profession.

As soon as he had reached his native shore, Christopher had begun looking about for a place to live. He had no particular place in mind. All he knew for certain was that he wanted to live in the country. During his stay in India, he had dreamed continually of England's green hills and smiling countryside, and he was eager to find a home now where his dream could be made a reality.

But in mid December, the countryside was not so smiling and the hills not so green as they had appeared in his dreams. In fact, as Christopher reflected wryly, they were damned bleak. The cold smote his bones after India's tropical heat, and he could not seem to keep warm in spite of woolen under-waistcoats, a knitted muffler, and a heavy greatcoat. He began to wonder if life in England was going to prove so very congenial after all.

This sense of being adrift in a hostile land was aggravated by his loneliness. He had no family left alive, and only a handful of friends, most of whom he had lost touch with over the years. Thus it had been with the utmost joy that he had met his old friend Roger Merrill when he was in London on business the week before.

Roger had recognized him immediately and hailed him with pleasure. They had stood for a long time chatting amid the foot traffic streaming past the City offices where they had met. When Christopher had mentioned he was looking for a place to settle, Roger had suggested Dorsetshire, his own home county.

"I've a property there near Yeovil, as snug a place as any in the kingdom. You could stay with us while you look about for a place of your own. Have you plans for over the holidays? No? Why, then, you must come to us for Christmas, to be sure. Yes, I must insist. My wife will be glad to have you, I know. No, you won't be putting us out a bit; we always have a house full of guests over Christmas."

It had sounded an attractive proposition to Christopher. At first he had demurred, saying he was sure his presence over the holidays must put Roger and his wife out, but Roger had protested against this idea with so much energy that, in the end, Christopher was brought to accept his invitation. With a joyful heart, he consented to spend the holidays at Roger's home in Dorsetshire.

He had been unable to accompany Roger down to Dorsetshire that day, having some business in London still to settle. But he had promised to come down as soon as he was able. Roger had assured him he would be welcome anytime he cared to come, and Christopher had parted from his friend feeling that England was not, perhaps, so bleak a place after all.

His business was quickly transacted, and he was ready to leave London by the following day. He had hired a post chaise and four fast horses and set out for Dorsetshire in high spirits. But as he had neared his destination, snow had begun to fall, until it grew difficult to see the road beneath its blanket of white. The post boys had looked grave and expressed doubt whether they could get through to Yeovil that night.

Christopher had not liked the idea of spending Christmas Eve in an inn. He knew from bitter experience how cheerless provincial inns could be, but there seemed no alternative. So at the next village they had come to, he had instructed the post boys to walk the horses up and down while he went to make inquiries about a suitable hostelry. He preferred to make these inquiries himself rather than entrusting them to the post boys, for he was resolved that if the inn were as squalid as some he had stayed at lately, he would press on to Yeovil in spite of the snow.

The village itself, at least, was not a squalid place. Christopher looked with appreciation at the neat square ranged round with quaint, peaked-roof shops, even as he shivered in the wind's icy blast. A few shops were still open, and the light from their windows threw welcoming patches of golden light onto the snowy pavement outside. At one of these, a grocer's, Christopher paused to survey the trays of figs, nuts, candied fruits, and other delicacies in the window. It struck him as quintessentially English, this display of good cheer and abundance. In a way, it embodied everything he had longed for during his exile in India.

As he stood reflecting on these themes, the shop door opened and a girl came out. Christopher looked after her as she hurried down the street. She was a pretty girl, slim and graceful-looking, with golden curls peeping beneath her bonnet and a soft color in her cheeks. He found himself thinking that she, too, seemed quintessentially English, like the display in the grocer's window. The idea even crossed his mind that once he was established someplace with a comfortable home and his affairs in order, he would not mind finding a girl like this to settle down with.

The thought had no sooner crossed Christopher's mind, however, than he laughed at himself. Of course he had no idea what the young lady he had just seen was really like. Her appearance had been attractive, but on further acquaintance she might prove to possess some fatal flaw. She might have a disagreeable temper, or be already engaged to some other man, or she might not even be a lady at all, belonging rather to that class of prosperous farmers and merchants who were able to give their daughters "advantages." Christopher told himself all this, but still he continued to stand on the sidewalk and look after the young lady until she disappeared from view.

Having watched her out of sight, he turned around to study the grocer's window once more and found to his discomfiture that he himself was being watched. A young man in an apron and breeches stood regarding him from only a few feet away. He had apparently been engaged in the business of fastening the shutters for the night, judging by the set of portable steps he carried, but at the moment he was merely standing, regarding Christopher with a look both curious and appraising.

It occurred to Christopher that this might be someone who could inform him about local hostelries. So he smiled at the young man and said, "Good evening. I wonder if you might be able to help me. I'm a stranger in these parts. I'm in need of lodging. Is there a decent inn somewhere hereabouts?"

The young man subjected him to another searching gaze—a gaze that had something critical in it. When he spoke, however, his voice was cordial. "Aye, the Bull's just around the corner there. It's a decent place, and Mrs. Merriweather will be able to put you up, I don't doubt."

Christopher thanked him, bestowed a generous tip upon him, then turned his steps toward the Bull. He was still resolved that if it were one of the dirty and derelict inns he had stayed in a few times during his previous travels, he would push on to Yeovil in spite of the post boys' dire predictions.

But the Bull proved a snug-looking hostelry of ivy-covered brick furnished forth with a profusion of chimneys. On the whole, Christopher was disposed to regard it with approval. So he hastened back to where the post boys were waiting and directed them to put up at the Bull for the night.

Mrs. Merriweather, the landlady of the Bull, welcomed him warmly and installed him in the inn's best bedchamber, a comfortable room with an old-fashioned four-poster bed and flowered chintz hangings. The dinner she presently laid before him was a very comfortable one, too.

By the time Christopher had eaten his fill of fricasseed sole, ham, boiled fowl, and baked apple dumpling, he was more than ever disposed to regard the Bull with favor.

He was weary from his long journey and decided to retire early. In his room, as he lay in the chintz-draped bed waiting for sleep to come, it struck him that the morrow was Christmas Day. He wondered if the snow would have subsided enough for him to push on to Yeovil, or if he would be forced to spend the whole day kicking his heels at the Bull.

Well, there are worse places I could spend the day, he reminded himself. *And at least I never committed to arriving at Roger's in time for Christmas. He won't be alarmed or disappointed if I'm not there. I'll just have to make the best of it, whatever happens.*

With this philosophical attitude, Christopher fell asleep. And so well did his philosophy serve him that when he awoke the next day and looked out the window, he was hardly disappointed to see snow was still falling steadily.

As he stood in his dressing gown looking out the window, an apple-cheeked maidservant came bustling into the room. "Merry Christmas, sir," she told him as she plumped down a can of hot water on his wash stand. "There's breakfast laid out in the small parlor, and dinner'll be served at three o'clock sharp. There's to be goose and sirloin of beef, two kinds of puddings, and a cake made according to Mrs. Merriweather's own special receipt."

Smiling, Christopher said he was sure everything would be delicious. The maidservant assented vigorously and went on in a confidential voice, "Mrs. Merriweather wanted me to ask you if you wouldn't care to take your dinner in the public room with the other gen-

·tlemen? Of course they're none of them Quality like you, but all very nice gentlemen with nothing low or common about them. She thought it might be more friendly for you, seeing it's Christmas and all. But she said it would be just as you pleased, sir, and if you preferred to take your dinner alone in the small parlor, there'd be no difficulty about it."

"Why, I should be very glad to have company," said Christopher. "By all means, let me dine in the public room with the others." Of all the disappointments connected with his interrupted journey, the thought of spending Christmas alone rather than surrounded by a gay throng at Roger's had been the greatest. The idea of companionship was so pleasant that he would have been willing to risk the experiment even without the maidservant's assurances that his companions were neither low nor common.

As it proved, however, the maidservant had been quite right. When Christopher went down to the public room at three o'clock, having whiled away the morning and early afternoon with reading and a chilly but invigorating walk, he found the gentlemen assembled there all perfect types of respectability. The local apothecary and doctor, both bachelors; a young schoolmaster, similarly unencumbered; an elderly widower whose children were all grown and living far away; a commercial traveler in imported wines who had been trapped by the storm like Christopher himself: all these were gathered about the Bull's festive board. They greeted Christopher with pleasure and proceeded to draw him into their circle at once.

"I hear you've been caught in the storm like me," said the commercial traveler, a rubicund gentleman by the name of Mr. Phipps. "A great nuisance, ain't it? But if one travels for a living, one learns to expect these lit-

tle inconveniences. I can only bless God that my wife is
the most understanding of women. It's too bad to fail
poor Clara on Christmas Day of all days, poor darling,
but she won't hold it against me, sir; she won't hold it
against me. I hope your wife is equally understanding?"

Smiling, Christopher said that he had no wife. He
was amused to find these words immediately brought to
mind the image of the golden-haired girl he had seen
outside the grocer's shop the evening before. "I was to
spend the holiday with a friend near Yeovil, but the
snow has made getting there impossible. Or so at least
the post boys assure me. Between you and me, I wonder
sometimes if the quality of our landlady's home brew
had not something to do with their disinclination to
press on!"

The doctor said positively that the post boys had
counseled him wisely, whatever their motives. "The road
between here and Yeovil always drifts badly, sir. I've seen
it as high as your head sometimes when there was no
more than a few inches of snow on the ground. It's as
well you decided to stay over rather than pushing on."

"Aye, and you'll find your lot has fallen in a goodly
place, sir," put in the schoolmaster in a sonorous voice.
"Mrs. Merriweather's a famous cook. You won't find a
better dinner anywhere than what she'll give us today."

Christopher was amused by this extravagant praise,
but by the time he had eaten his way through three
courses, composed of turtle soup, stewed eels, fried
whiting, roast goose, serpent of mutton, sirloin of beef,
mashed potatoes, boiled beetroot, curd fritters, cheese-
cake, custard, mince pie, and plum pudding, he was disposed to echo it.

"An excellent dinner," he told Mrs. Merriweather as
he brushed the last crumbs of plum pudding from his
mouth and settled back in his chair with a sigh of reple-

tion. "A real old English Christmas dinner, just as I remembered it."

Mrs. Merriweather beamed and said she was sure she was much obliged to Mr. Garret for his kind words. "And now, if you'd like to step into the taproom, sir, there's a good fire burning, and I've made up a batch of my famous rack punch. If I do say so myself, sir, there's nobody as makes a rack punch like me. It's an old receipt, which my mother passed to me from *her* mother, under pledge of darkest secrecy."

The punch proved eminently drinkable, whatever its secrets, and the six men who were gathered in the taproom drank a glass to Mrs. Merriweather's health with right goodwill. "Oh, this is excellent," said Christopher, allowing his glass to be refilled and settling back in an armchair with a sigh. "I've dreamed of punch like this and a dinner like this the whole time I've been out of England."

"Been abroad, have you?" said the apothecary. "Thought your complexion was a bit darkish for this place and season. East Indies, is it, or West?"

Christopher explained about his stay in India and how he had retired from his business there to return to his native land. "I've been looking about for a place to settle, but haven't had much luck finding what I'm looking for. In fact, that's part of the reason I was traveling to Yeovil. My friend who lives there thought I might be able to find a property in the area to suit me. But once again I've had bad luck—such bad luck, in fact, that I haven't even been able to get there!"

"Ah, but who's to say that wasn't *good* luck?" said the elderly widower portentously. "The workings of Providence are mysterious indeed, sir, as you'll realize when you've lived as many years as I have. Perhaps now you've seen our neighborhood, you'll find you'd rather settle here than go on to Yeovil."

There were cries of acclaim at this suggestion, and several of the other gentlemen began to adduce reasons why Christopher would be much better off staying in this neighborhood rather than traveling farther abroad. "And I know just the place for you, sir," the doctor told him, gesturing broadly with his glass of punch. "There's a very nice property just a mile or two beyond the village here that I happen to know is standing empty. It'd be just the thing for you."

"Of course! The old Bradley place. Wyngate, that is," agreed the apothecary. "You're quite right, Mr. Pettijohn. That would be just the place for Mr. Garret."

Christopher found their parochial loyalty amusing, but he had drunk several glasses of punch and was willing to humor them. "What sort of a place is Wyngate?" he asked.

The descriptions that ensued were not very clear, but clear enough to convince Christopher that if one half of them were true, Wyngate was a perfect paradise on earth. "If it's as wonderful as all that, why isn't someone living there now?" he asked skeptically. "From what Mr. Pettijohn said"—he bowed to the doctor—"it's standing empty, and from what *you* said"—he looked at the schoolmaster—"I gather it's been unoccupied for several years now. That seems to show something must be wrong with it."

"No, it's only that when old Mrs. Bradley died, there was a difficulty about her will," explained the apothecary. "For the last ten years, the place has been tied up in a lawsuit while the heirs fought over it. But the lawsuit was settled just last month, and now the place is up for sale. My cousin works over at the land office in Carville, so I know all about it."

Christopher shook his head dubiously. "But if the place has stood empty for ten years, then it stands to reason it won't be in very good shape," he said. "Ten years is a long time for a building to stand unoccupied. If it hasn't gone entirely to wrack and ruin in that time, I daresay it must be well on its way."

"It might have if anybody but Robert Fowler had the care of it," agreed the apothecary. "But old Fowler's a conscientious soul. I'd bet five pounds the place is in as good a shape now as when he took charge of it."

"Robert Fowler's the caretaker," explained the doctor. "He's something of a crank, but his worst enemy couldn't accuse him of being derelict in his duties."

They all seemed so positive on this point that Christopher was driven to his last defense. "Yes, but even if Wyngate is all you say it is, it may be beyond my purse," he said. "In fact, if it is even half as wonderful as you describe, then I am sure it must be."

"Well, it wouldn't hurt to at least see," said the doctor. "Sam's cousin over at the land office could tell you in a trice."

"But the land office wouldn't be open today. It would mean staying over an extra day, just on the chance the place might suit me. And my friend is expecting me in Yeovil. Much as your descriptions tempt me, I think I must decline."

Here his companions broke into a perfect babble of argument, trying to convince him he would regret it forever if he did not at least look at Wyngate. In the midst of this argument, an elderly man came quietly into the taproom and seated himself at the bar. It took several minutes for Christopher's companions to notice him, but when they did, they hailed him with loud expressions of delight. "Why, of all the timely apparitions!

Here's the very man we've been wanting, regularly johnny-on-the-spot. Hi, Fowler, come over and have a glass of punch and help us convince Mr. Garret that Wyngate would be just the place for him."

Chapter 4

Robert Fowler was much surprised to be hailed by such gentlemen as Mr. Pettijohn the doctor and Mr. Leonard who kept the school. He came over to their table slowly and a little suspiciously, unable to make out what they wanted of him. "Fowler, you're just the man we've been looking for," said Mr. Pettijohn. "This is Mr. Garret. Tell him that Wyngate's as fine a property as he'll find in England."

"Tell him he'll always regret it if he doesn't at least look at the place," urged Mr. Bledsoe, the widower from over Carville way. "I'm sure the Bradleys can't be asking much of a price for it. It stands to reason they'll be eager to have the place off their hands now the lawsuit is settled."

"Tell him what fine orchards there are at Wyngate, and how the gardens grow the best vegetables in the village," instructed Mr. Stirling, the apothecary. "Indeed, I'd buy the place myself if I had the brass to do it."

It took Robert a little while to decipher all this talk, but he finally made out that the "him" referred to was the young gentleman with the brown complexion who sat in their midst, wearing an embarrassed smile. Robert gathered the gentleman was a stranger to the area who was looking for a property to buy.

Ever since the lawsuit had been settled, Robert had lived in fear that Wyngate would be sold to a new owner who would promptly turn him out and hire servants of his own. But today he faced the idea squarely and found it no longer had the power to frighten him. What, after all, did he have to dread? He had money enough in the bank to keep him the rest of his life, even if he did lose his place.

And now that he had made his peace with the sister he loved and the nephew he was only just coming to know, he need never fear dwindling into a lonely old age. In a burst of charitable spirit, he decided the young gentleman was welcome to buy Wyngate if he wanted to. He, Robert, would take his chances that there would be a place for him no matter who might own it. So he essayed a cautious smile at Christopher and said, "Indeed, sir, what the gentlemen say is nothing but the truth. Wyngate's a fine property—as fine a property as you'll find in the whole of England, upon my word."

Christopher said politely that he was sure this was true. "But I'd have to stay over an extra day if I want to see the place," he explained. "And I'm really supposed to be spending the holidays at a friend's in Yeovil. In fact, if it hadn't been for being snowed in, I'd be there this minute."

Robert thought this over. "But you're here now," he pointed out. "And there's no need to stay over till tomorrow, sir, if it's only a look at the place you want. I'm going that way myself this evening, once I finish my pint. You're welcome to come along with me if you like.

You can poke around the house and grounds a bit, and if you think the place might suit you, you can be seeing the agent at Carville tomorrow and doing the thing properly."

The doctor, the apothecary, and the other gentlemen were loud in acclaim of this suggestion. Before long, in spite of Christopher's protests, he found himself bundled once more in his overcoat and muffler and walking along the lane that led to Wyngate, accompanied by all six of his new friends.

He had no expectation that the property would really suit him. He told himself it would be entirely too opportune to run across the home of his dreams in such a serendipitous manner. But when he first beheld Wyngate, flanked by clusters of plumy hemlocks with its orchard stretching out behind it, all he could say was "Yes—oh, yes," in a fervent voice.

"Just you wait till you see the inside, sir," Robert told him with proprietary pride. "*And* the gardens and orchard. They're a regular treat in the spring and summer. Still, even in the winter, you can get an idea of what the property's like. Take a look around, sir. I think you'll agree it's something out of the common way."

Looking about the neat and well-kept grounds, Christopher could only give voice to the most sincere agreement. And when he penetrated inside the house and saw the elegance of its public apartments, the convenience of its domestic offices, and the solid comfort of its bedchambers, he realized that here, indeed, was the place he wished to set up his rest.

It was merely a question now of whether he could afford to. And on the whole, he thought he could. The style of the property was elegant without being extravagant, and though there were some acres of forest and farmland attached to the house and its immediate grounds, it was certainly not a grand estate. Christopher was sure it would be well within his budget. All in all, the place could not have suited him better if it had been made especially for him. And to think he might never have found it if it had not been snowing and the grocer's boy had not directed him to the Bull!

"It's a wonderful place," said Christopher. "I shall certainly stay over another day and see the agent at Carville."

His companions all clapped him on the back and told him this decision showed great good sense. They then escorted him back to the Bull and joined him in demolishing the remains of the goose and cold beef left over from dinner.

The next day early, Christopher presented himself at the land office in Carville to inquire about buying Wyngate. The agent, barely concealing his delight at the prospect of a handsome commission, undertook to answer all his questions about the property. So satisfactory was the result of these inquiries that when Christopher returned to the Bull late that afternoon, he had already paid down a sum of money to hold the property in his name, the remainder of the money to be transferred by his London banker when the necessary legal formalities had been completed.

The snow had ceased by now, and a wintry sun was slipping toward the western horizon as Christopher drove into the innyard of the Bull. He learned from the ostler that the wine merchant, Mr. Phipps, had taken advantage of the weather's clearing to travel on toward his home and his long-suffering wife. But his other companions of the previous day were gathered around the hearth when he entered the taproom, and when they learned the result of his business, they one and all insisted on shaking his hand and welcoming him formally to the neighborhood.

Dinner was served not long after this. Christopher chose to dine once more with the other gentlemen in the public room rather than taking his meal in the private parlor. After dinner, they retired to the taproom again, where Christopher stood them a round to celebrate his new status as landowner.

The taproom was a good deal busier than on the previous evening. A great many farmers and other country folk had dropped in to drink a pint and talk over the day's events. Later in the evening, a group of gentlemen came in together, laughing and talking among themselves as they shook the snow from their boots and removed gloves, mufflers, and overcoats.

"By Jove, I'd almost forgotten it was whist night," said Mr. Pettijohn, looking toward this group. "There's a standing game here at the Bull every Friday evening. Are you a whist player by any chance, Mr. Garret? If so, I'll introduce you to Mr. Winwood." The doctor nodded toward a fair-haired young man who was talking to an elderly gentleman near the taproom door. "He helped form the club a year or so ago, and I'm sure he'd be glad to add you to the list of members if you were interested in joining."

Christopher did play whist, and he welcomed the idea of a friendly game to while away the evening. Together he and the good doctor shouldered their way through the crowd. When they reached the group of whist players, Mr. Pettijohn set about introducing him to Mr. Gregory Winwood, the president of the Village Whist Society.

There proved no difficulty at all about securing

membership to this amiable society. Mr. Winwood declared he and the other members were honored to welcome the future owner of Wyngate to the fold. "We're very glad to have you, Mr. Garret," he said, shaking Christopher's hand warmly. "So you're just back from India, hey? I'll wager old England seems pretty tame after wrestling with elephants and man-eating tigers over there."

Christopher explained that he had had little experience with elephants and tigers, his business in India having been confined to the more settled and civilized portions of the country. Mr. Winwood seemed a little disappointed to hear this, but nonetheless insisted Christopher sit at his table and partner him in the first rubber. When Christopher helped him win it through the clever playing of a queen, he was more than ever inclined to look on him with favor.

"By Jove, that was smart work, old fellow," he told Christopher as he gathered up the cards. "A fortunate thing for me that you're my partner!"

"I consider the good fortune to be mine," Christopher told him frankly. "This was looking to be a dull evening before you were good enough to take pity on me. Mind you, I have nothing to say against Mrs. Merriweather and her hospitality. Both have been excellent in their way, but you know it's slow work, putting in one's evenings at an inn."

"I suppose it is," agreed Mr. Winwood. He paused to shuffle the cards, then spoke again in a reflective voice. "Are you going to be staying at the Bull much longer?"

"At least another day or two, I think. There are still some details concerning the sale of the property that must be attended to."

"Why, then, you must to come to our party tomorrow

night," said Mr. Winwood, shuffling the cards a final time and bringing them together with a snap. "That will while away at least one of your evenings. My parents give a party every year on December twenty-seventh, and this year it's sort of a combination Christmas and engagement party because I've just gotten engaged."

He spoke these words with such evident pride that Christopher was amused, yet a little envious as well. It was easy to see that Mr. Winwood thought the sun rose and set in his fiancée. His descriptions certainly made her sound a paragon, although half of Christopher's interest was lost when he learned she was a brunette. He had nothing against dark beauties, of course, but he had seen little else while he was in India, and he found now that his own vision of ideal womanhood tended toward the fair. Something like the blond girl he had seen outside the grocery the other night. . . .

Mr. Winwood, meanwhile, was going on with descriptions of his Cecelia. "So she and I thought we might as well make the announcement tomorrow night, since most of our friends and family will be there. I'd be very pleased if you could come, too, Garret. We'd be honored to have you join us."

Chrisptopher protested, saying that he as a stranger would certainly be out of place in such a gathering. Mr. Winwood waved these protests aside, however. "Nonsense, man, you're not a stranger, you're a neighbor— or will be, as soon as you take possession of Wyngate. I give you my word you won't be out of place at all. Yes, and it'll be a fine opportunity for you to meet the local gentry. We have some very pretty girls who live hereabouts," he added slyly.

Whether it was these words that turned the trick, or Mr. Winwood's previous assurances, Christopher could not have said, but he found himself accepting the invitation with heartfelt pleasure. Mr. Winwood repeated that he, his parents, and his fiancée would be very glad to have him, and, having given him instructions about how to get to the Winwoods' home, they parted late that evening on the best of terms.

Chapter 5

Christmas Day in the Roswell household had been celebrated in a fashion familiar to Ellie since she was a little girl.

She had risen early and eaten a festive breakfast with her parents and younger brothers and sisters. There were sausages and broiled fish, chops and rashers of bacon, boiled eggs, muffins, marmalade, and hothouse grapes in addition to the usual toast, hot rolls, and cold meat. Ellie's brothers and sisters could hardly eat for excitement—or so they said—but the food disappeared in prodigious quantities nonetheless, washed down with tea and accompanied by the buzz of excited conversation.

After breakfast, the whole family went off to church to hear the Christmas service read. The local music society sang, and the local vicar delivered an earnest homily on the meaning of the season.

"And so let us emulate He who was born this day, and let our light shine forth before men, with faith in God above and with our hands extended in help and fellowship to our neighbors," he finished, settling his spectacles on his nose and beaming in a nearsighted way at the congregation.

Ellie, as she rose for the final hymn and benediction, found her thoughts dwelling on the vicar's final words. She could not flatter herself that she had done much in the way of helping her neighbors that year. Only that goose she had sent to the Beales could qualify as a real act of charity, and considering she had been half regretting her impulsive action ever since committing it, she feared even that was of dubious value.

I still can't help wishing I had that shawl, she told herself. *But it's better that the Beales should have a goose for Christmas. I know it is. I'll just try to think of that and not the shawl.*

With such thoughts as these did Ellie comfort herself for the remainder of the service. Afterward, she joined with the rest of the congregation in shaking hands and wishing her friends and neighbors a merry Christmas. This done, the family returned to their home, where there were gifts for the small brothers and sisters and a few for Ellie herself.

A multitude of dolls, storybooks, lead soldiers, wooden animals, sugarplums, and gingerbread were shortly scattered over the parlor carpet, having been brought forth by the elder Roswells and rejoiced over by the younger ones. For the next few hours, Ellie was kept so busy helping to dress dolls, assemble puzzles, march animals into toy Noah's arks, and read *History of the Robins* and *Jack Dandy's Delight* to her importunate siblings that she had no time for thoughts of shawls.

The highlight of the day was Christmas dinner, over which Mrs. Roswell, the cook, and all the maids had been jointly slaving for the past twenty-four hours. A traditional boar's head, festooned in greenery and featuring an apple clenched in its jaws, was the mainstay of the feast, together with turkey, goose, and a joint of beef. These dishes were amply reinforced by a multitude of others. Stuffed onions, carrots in cream, mashed potatoes, parsnip fritters, spinach gratin, and turnip custard were handsomely served forth in unstinted quantities, not to mention an eye-popping assembly of pies, puddings, creams, and jellies. The meal concluded, as usual, with Mrs. Roswell urging everyone in the family to eat a helping of mince pie. "If you eat mince pie every day of the Christmas Season, it'll bring you good luck in the year ahead," she told them firmly.

"Oh, Mother, that's pure superstition!" protested Ellie, laughing. "You can't really believe that, or expect us to believe it, either." Nonetheless, she ate mince pie along with the others, reflecting that possibly, just possibly, there might be something in the old superstition.

With Christmas Day all but over, the Winwoods' ball on the twenty-seventh was looming large, and Ellie was beginning to feel very nervous about it. She could not forget that there would be people there who would know of her past connection with Gregory, including Gregory himself. She would have to carry her head high and show by every look and word that his marrying Cecelia Lake did not disturb her in the least.

Ellie felt this would have been much easier if she were wearing that shawl from Miss Asher's. Anyone might carry her head high to appear in such a stylish and handsome garment. Still, she could not really regret that she had spent her guinea as she had. It was pleasant to think of the Beales' surprise when they received their goose on Christmas Eve. Ellie hugged the thought to herself, and found in it a comfort nearly equal to the happiness of owning a real imitation Indian shawl.

There was further comfort in reflecting that even if

she had bought the shawl, she might not have been able to wear it. In addition to her other gifts that Christmas, she had been surprised to receive an exquisite lace cloak with swansdown trimming from her mother and father. "You're a good girl, Ellie," her mother had said, as Ellie had exclaimed over this gift and protested she was too old to be receiving Christmas presents. "I know you're not a child anymore, but your father and I thought you deserved something. The milliner over in Carville says these are all the rage for young girls this Season. I thought it would be just the thing for you to wear to the Winwoods' party."

Ellie was pleased by the cloak, which was indeed a very pretty thing. In its way it was as pretty as the shawl, although Ellie could not help feeling the shawl was the more dashing of the two garments. The cloak, after all, was white like her new evening dress, and though dressing all in white was perfectly unexceptionable for a young lady, Ellie could not help feeling it was rather unsophisticated for a girl who had achieved the mature age of twenty-one. The shawl, on the other hand, with its rich-dyed hues, would have stamped her immediately as a woman of taste and discretion. But parents were often slow to recognize that their children were growing up, as Ellie reflected philosophically. They had meant well in giving her the cloak, and she had no wish to hurt their feelings by seeming to disparage it. Accordingly, she thanked them for their gift and blessed heaven she had not to make up her mind between wearing it and the shawl to the Winwoods' party.

On the afternoon of the great day, Ellie began very early to make her preparations. First of all, she rang for hot water and bathed and washed her hair. It took some time for her hair to dry, but once this had been accomplished she arranged it carefully in a cloud of ringlets, modeled after one of the illustrations in her mother's fashion magazine. Trimmed with a spray of white silk roses, she thought it very becoming, though she could not help being a little sorry she had not dark hair instead of blonde. It appeared from the magazine that the fashion for blondes was quite done with. Ellie reflected bitterly that it was highly unjust for a fashion magazine to make such sweeping statements. One could hardly change one's hair coloring as one changed one's skirt length or sleeve style, after all!

Fortunately, before Ellie could become very bitter on the subject, her littlest sister, who had been watching her beauty preparations with rapt attention, exclaimed, "Oh, Ellie, you do have the prettiest hair! It shines just like gold in the light."

This soothed Ellie's feelings somewhat, and they were further soothed when she slipped into her new dress of white net over satin. It really was a lovely dress, even if she had made it herself, and she had the comfortable certainty that it was in the highest kick of fashion. If only she could have had the shawl to wear over it! That touch of vivid crimson and gold would have made a striking contrast against the dress's pristine white. But the lace cloak gave a nice effect, too, rather like frostwork against a background of snow.

And when another of her sisters declared, "You look beautiful, Ellie. I'll bet you'll be the prettiest girl at the party," Ellie did not feel she was overstating the case by much.

Her mother, too, was appreciative when Ellie came downstairs to show herself in full dress. "You look very lovely, dear. I don't believe I ever saw you in better looks. Would you like to borrow my pearls to wear tonight?"

"Oh, but I thought *you* would want to wear your

pearls, Mama," said Ellie with surprise. Mrs. Roswell's string of pearls was the only real jewelry in the family, and Ellie had assumed as a matter of course that her mother would want to wear it herself for such an important occasion.

"No, I shall wear the locket your papa gave me for Christmas," said Mrs. Roswell, caressing that ornament where it rested against her slender throat. "Not only is it very pretty, it has a great deal of meaning for me, since all of you children have given me a bit of your hair to put in it."

Seeing that her mother was in earnest about preferring the locket, Ellie was glad enough to accept the pearls for herself. They added quite a distinguishing touch to her toilette, she felt. *Of course it would be better if they were diamonds or sapphires or emeralds,* she told herself. *Sparkling stones are so much more elegant and dashing than pearls. But since I did not even reckon on having pearls an hour ago, I ought not to complain.*

Indeed, she was not inclined to complain about anything as she wrapped her woolen cloak over her lace one and went out to the carriage with her parents. Her brothers and sisters, all of whom were still too young to attend a grown-up party, looked on wistfully as they drove away. Ellie waved and blew kisses to them, reflecting that up till a few years ago she, too, had been an envious onlooker to these proceedings. Now she was old enough to accompany her parents to the Winwoods', and she told herself she ought to be properly cognizant of her good fortune. Still, she could not help feeling a little nervous at the prospect of the evening ahead, in spite of the consciousness of being elegantly coiffed and fashionably dressed and on her way to the premier party of the season.

The carriage had not far to go. In point of fact, the

Roswells lived next door to the Winwoods, so that going from one house to the other involved merely going down the Roswell drive, down the lane a rod or two, then turning into the Winwoods' drive. It was a distance easily covered on foot, but Mrs. Roswell maintained that it was not fitting to go even a short distance on foot while in evening dress, and so the carriage was called into service and the horses harnessed for what was less than a five-minute drive.

Ellie was in a positive flutter of nerves as the carriage slowed to a stop before the Winwoods' house. She tried to calm herself as she followed her parents up the steps and accompanied her mother to the ladies' cloakroom to remove her outer garments and change her fur-lined slippers for satin ones. A peep in the glass served to somewhat restore her composure. Her hair was just as satisfactory as before and her dress just as pretty. She gave a twitch or two to the lace cloak across her shoulders, a final smooth to her net and satin skirts, then told her mother she was ready. Together they stepped across the hall toward the saloon where the Winwoods always held their parties.

The first person Ellie saw on entering the room was Cecelia Lake, wearing the shawl she herself had admired so much at Miss Asher's.

There really could be no mistake. As soon as Ellie's first dazed shock had worn off, she was able to look at it more closely and make sure of it beyond any possible doubt. It was certainly the identical shawl, and Cecelia was certainly wearing it. She looked quite handsome in it, too, as Ellie enviously reflected. The rich scarlet and gold admirably became her brunette coloring, which was likewise set off by a dress of saffron-colored silk. Ellie felt she must look quite dull and colorless in comparison.

But it was too late to do anything about that now,

even if that had been possible. Already Mrs. Winwood was sweeping down on her and her parents with exclamations of pleasure. There was nothing to do but pin a smile on her lips and greet her hostess in return with as much gaiety as she could feign.

She heroically bore her part in the flurry of greetings that ensued, even when it came time to shake hands with Gregory. "Don't you look pretty tonight, Miss Roswell," he said, and Ellie was able to smile at him quite naturally and say, "Thank you, Mr. Winwood. You are very kind, I'm sure."

"You know Cecelia, of course," he said, glancing toward his fiancée with pride. Seeing his look, Cecelia came forward and smiled sweetly at Ellie as she dropped a curtsy.

"Good evening, Miss Roswell," she said in her soft, lisping voice.

Ellie wished her a good evening in return. They chatted for a few minutes, and in the process Ellie was able to ascertain that Cecelia was as hen-witted as she remembered. Still, it was impossible to really dislike her. Her smile was as sweet and ingenuous as a child's, and when she exclaimed over Ellie's dress and said she looked perfectly lovely in it, it was evident she meant the words sincerely.

"Well, you look very lovely, too, Miss Lake," said Ellie, feeling such generosity deserved a response in kind. "I have been admiring your dress ever since I came in. And your shawl, too . . . did you get it at Miss Asher's? I thought so. I was sure I could not be mistaken. I noticed that shawl in particular because I thought it the very prettiest one of all."

"Thank you," said Cecelia, flushing with satisfaction. "I thought so, too. I am so glad you admire it, Miss Roswell."

At that point Gregory, who had excused himself to talk to another acquaintance, came drifting over again, causing Ellie to say she had better be rejoining her parents. "Oh, but it's been delightful to talk to you, Miss Roswell," said Cecelia with the same childlike sincerity.

"Aye, we're glad you could come, Miss Roswell," said Gregory warmly. "Perhaps you'll do me the honor of standing up with me for one of the dances later on?"

"Thank you, I would enjoy that very much, Mr. Winwood," said Ellie. Having arranged with him to dance the third set of dances together, she took leave of the newly engaged couple and went over to sit with her mother and father.

She supposed the whole thing had gone off pretty well. Indeed, when she examined her heart, she was amazed to find that she had lost the rankling sense of resentment she had felt ever since Gregory had taken up with Cecelia. Cecelia might not be an intellectual woman, but she was sweet and good-humored and obviously very much in love with him.

Now that she thought about it, she realized Gregory wasn't exactly an intellectual giant himself. But he, too, was very good-natured, and likely he and Cecelia would deal excellently well together. All in all, Ellie felt she could observe their happiness without resenting it any longer.

If she was inclined to resent anything, it was the loss of the shawl. Yet even here, she found herself sustaining her loss with philosophical resignation. She had known when she spent the guinea on the goose that she was probably losing any chance of ever possessing the shawl herself. Certainly she did not regret her decision. But it was a strange twist of fate to see it now on her rival's back. Ellie could not help wondering a little uneasily what other unsuspected chains of circumstances she had set in motion by her impulsive good deed.

Just then she felt a tap on her shoulder.

"Miss Roswell? There is someone I would like to introduce to you."

Turning around, Ellie beheld Mrs. Winwood, her hostess, with a broad smile on her face. By her side was a gentleman Ellie had never seen before. Such at least was her first impression, although when she looked at him again she was conscious of an indefinable sense of familiarity.

Ellie decided, with a touch of whimsy, that it was merely because he was so completely the embodiment of all her dreams. He was tall with dark hair and dark eyes and a singularly handsome though rather sunbrowned face, and he was looking at her with something approaching reverence in his expression. Ellie dropped her eyes, feeling both flattered and embarrassed.

"Miss Roswell, this is Mr. Garret," said Mrs. Winwood. "You haven't met him yet, have you? Ah, I suspected as much. It's no surprise you haven't met him before, for it happens he's just back from India. But you'll be glad to hear he has decided to settle in our neighborhood, so we may all look forward to seeing a good deal of him in the future. Mr. Garret, this is Miss Roswell. She and her parents live right next door to us, in that big half-timbered place with all the gables."

The young man made no response to this. He was still staring at Ellie with the same bemused expression. Mrs. Winwood gave an amused chuckle. "Look at that, Miss Roswell! You've knocked him so cock-a-hoop that he's clean forgotten his manners. I don't know what the custom is in India, Mr. Garret, but here in England when one's introduced to a lady, it's usual to at least say 'how-d'ye-do.'"

"Yes, to be sure," said the young man, coloring. "How do you do, Miss Roswell, and I beg you will forgive me. Indeed, I am very pleased to make your acquaintance."

"That's better," said Mrs. Winwood approvingly. "But don't just ask her pardon, Mr. Garret. Ask her to dance. That's the way to win a lady's favor, not stand there staring at her like a Noddy."

"Yes, of course," said the young man. There was laughter in his eyes now, and an engaging smile on his lips as he looked at Ellie. "Will you dance with me, Miss Roswell?" he asked.

"Yes, of course," said Ellie, smiling back at him. She felt all of a flutter and yet strangely calm, as though something she had long expected was finally coming to pass.

The center of the saloon had been cleared for dancing, and the fiddlers were just striking up the first dance as Ellie accompanied Christopher onto the floor. They stood looking at each other as they took their places in the set, waiting for the top couple to lead off. After a moment, Christopher spoke with a rueful smile on his face. "You must be thinking me very rag-mannered," he said. "Indeed, I am not normally so gauche, Miss Roswell. But when Mrs. Winwood introduced me to you just now, it caught me rather off my guard. You see, I have seen you before."

"Have you?" said Ellie with amazement.

"Yes, just the other night, though you probably wouldn't remember." Christopher gave an embarrassed laugh. "It wasn't a proper meeting—indeed, I don't think you even saw me, though I certainly noticed you. But given the circumstances, it's not surprising you wouldn't remember anything about it."

"I don't *think* I do," said Ellie. "Although I did think there was something familiar about you when I first saw you, Mr. Garret. But indeed, I am sure I would remember if we had ever met before." She glanced up at him shyly.

Christopher smiled. "It would have been merely a glimpse, not a formal introduction," he said. "I was standing outside the grocer's on Christmas Eve, and I saw you come out of the shop. At least I think it was you—but no, I am sure it was. I could not be mistaken." He looked earnestly into Ellie's face.

"On Christmas Eve? Oh, yes, it was I," said Ellie, smiling as she recalled the reason for her presence at the grocer's. "What a very strange coincidence!"

"Very strange indeed," said Christopher gravely.

Chapter 6

During the dance, Christopher explained to Ellie how he had just returned from India. He went on to describe how he had gone searching for a house and how he had come to see and buy Wyngate.

"Oh, but that is wonderful news!" exclaimed Ellie, looking at him in awe. "To think you have bought Wyngate! You must know it has gone to my heart to think of the place standing vacant all these years. I always thought it the most charming house in the world."

"And I feel just the same," said Christopher.

As the dance went on, they discovered a number of other tastes in common. Indeed, they were getting on so well that when the dance ended, Christopher immediately asked Ellie to stand up with him a second time. During this dance they discussed music and books and poetry, finding yet more tastes in common, so that it was a wrench for Ellie to have to refuse him when he asked her to stand up with him a third time.

"Mama does not like me to dance with the same gentleman more than twice," she explained sadly. "She thinks it is not proper."

Christopher looked crestfallen. "Isn't it?" he said. "I did not know. Forgive me, Miss Roswell. I did not mean to urge you to contravene any rules of etiquette. I was simply having such a good time that I did not wish it to stop. I wonder . . . do you think it would be permissible if I sat and talked with you, even if we cannot dance any more?"

Ellie thought it would be all right. "And you could also take me in to supper if you wished," she suggested, with a shy sideways look at him. "There will be a sit-down supper at eleven o'clock in the dining room."

Christopher said he would like nothing better than to take her in to supper. He then accompanied her to a comfortable sofa a little distance from the crowd and settled down to continue their talk.

But alas, he had not calculated on Ellie's popularity. First one young man and then another came up and asked her to dance. If Ellie had been a London beauty diverting herself at Almack's Assembly Rooms, she might have felt no compunction about rejecting these offers, but such conduct was not to be thought of at the Winwoods' Christmas ball. Not only would Mrs. Winwood be offended, so would her other suitors, most of whom were young men Ellie had known all her life. So she was obliged to excuse herself frequently to Christopher and take to the dance floor for the space of twenty minutes at a time.

Ellie found this frustrating, the more so because it was such a ridiculous twist of fate. As a rule she was popular enough at dancing parties, but there had been occasions in the past when she had been obliged to sit out a dance or two because no suitable partner had presented himself. One of her fears in coming to the party that evening was that she would be left sitting forlornly on the sidelines while Gregory and Cecelia whirled about in each other's arms. Now she found herself positively besieged with partners and wishing only to sit quietly on the sidelines!

But I won't be foolish enough to complain about what is only a surfeit of good, she told herself, resignedly rising to her feet as yet another gentleman asked her to dance. Aloud, she told Christopher, "Indeed, Mr. Garret, why do you not dance, too? I hate to think of your sitting here cooling your heels all evening. You may as well enjoy yourself while you are here. It's obvious we shall have no chance to talk properly till supper anyway."

"I suppose not," he said, getting reluctantly to his feet. "And it's true I ought to do my duty by my hostess on the dance floor. But I warn you I shall be at your side directly as soon as suppertime comes."

"Why 'warn'?" inquired Ellie, smiling. "My dear Mr. Garret, I am looking forward to having supper with you!"

"That's good," said Christopher seriously. "Because I am looking forward to it, too. And if you were hoping to foist me off on some other lady, then you would be doomed to disappointment."

He smiled at her, a warm smile that kindled a glow in Ellie's heart. She gave him a quick, shy smile in return, then accepted her partner's arm and went out to disport herself on the dance floor with a heart as light as her heels.

Over her partner's shoulder, she watched Christopher as he went up to Mrs. Winwood and asked her to dance. Mrs. Winwood was clearly pleased with this invitation, and Ellie watched contentedly as they took their places on the floor. But she was a good deal less content when she saw him taking the floor with Cecelia Lake for the next dance.

Of course Cecelia is the guest of honor this evening, Ellie reminded herself. *It's only right that Mr. Garret should ask her to dance. He is merely doing the polite thing and showing that he has nice manners.* Still, she found the sight of Cecelia and Christopher together depressing. It was not that she herself had any claim on him, as she reminded herself. She had only met him this evening, and though he was undoubtedly a very attractive, engaging, amiable gentleman, still she did not mean to be silly. The future would show whether he had serious intentions or not. At present, he was welcome to dance with whomever he pleased. But still Ellie found comfort in reflecting that Cecelia was out of the running so far as Christopher Garret was concerned. That was yet another twist in this queerest of queer evenings: that she should actually be glad Cecelia was engaged to Gregory Winwood!

Fortunately Ellie had not long to wait before she obtained a much more substantial form of comfort. Mrs. Winwood announced that supper was ready, and before Ellie could wonder where Christopher was, he had appeared at her side, extending his arm to her with a smile.

"There you are," he said. "Together again at last! It seems an age since we parted." He stopped, frowning. "That sounds like hyperbole, doesn't it? The kind of thing any gazetted flirt might say. And yet I mean it most sincerely. It's strange, isn't it?" He threw Ellie a diffident look. "But there, perhaps I'm presuming. Perhaps you don't feel the thing I'm talking about."

"Oh, yes, I do," said Ellie, and for a little while forgot all about Cecelia Lake in a surge of pure, overwhelming happiness.

She remembered Cecelia later, however, as they were

sitting in the dining room eating their supper. The future Mrs. Winwood was sitting in the midst of a laughing group with her husband-to-be at her side and her shawl very much in evidence.

Ellie no longer envied her Gregory, but she still felt a little envious about the shawl. She sighed faintly, then looked up to find Christopher's eyes upon her.

"You are looking very serious, Miss Roswell," he said with a smile. "A penny for your thoughts?"

"I was admiring Miss Lake's toilette," said Ellie frankly. "She looks very lovely this evening."

"Does she?" said Christopher. "And who is Miss Lake?"

Ellie regarded him with amazement. "But you must know Miss Lake," she said. "She is the guest of honor, Gregory Winwood's fiancée. You were dancing with her only a few minutes ago. Surely you must remember? The pretty dark-haired girl with the yellow dress and red shawl?"

"Oh, yes, I do remember now. I suppose she is a pretty girl. I was thinking of someone else at the time, and so I am afraid paid scant attention."

The look that accompanied these words brought the color to Ellie's cheeks. It also banished from her heart the last vestige of envy. "Oh, but I do think Cecelia is a lovely girl," she protested. "I have always thought she had the prettiest hair—and dark hair is so fashionable right now."

"I'm afraid I don't care much for fashion, then," said Christopher. "To my mind your hair is much prettier than hers."

This compliment, and the look that accompanied it, threw Ellie into further confusion. "Oh! Well, I am sure I thank you very much, Mr. Garret," she said.

"You are very welcome," he said gravely, and added in a lower voice, "Indeed, I don't think there's a lady in the room who can hold a candle to you. From the first moment you walked into the room, I couldn't take my eyes off you. There's something about a woman all in white . . . especially a fair woman like yourself. It gives you a touch of the angelic. Especially with this lacy business over your shoulders." Gently he touched a fold of Ellie's lace cloak. "Very pretty. I like it much better than that hideous shawl your Miss Lake is wearing."

Ellie felt her jaw dropping. With an effort she pulled it up again and endeavored to look as though she had not been staggered by this casual statement. "Indeed?" she said, rather faintly. "You think her shawl hideous, then?"

"Indeed, yes," said Christopher with an emphatic nod. "No one who has seen real India work could confuse it for anything but a very bad imitation. Mind you, textiles were one of the things I dealt with while working for my uncle, so perhaps I may be something of a fanatic on the subject." He gave her a deprecating smile. "To speak truth, I'm afraid that was the thing I chiefly remarked while dancing with Miss Lake—that she was wearing a travesty of an Indian shawl. As such, I hardly remarked her hair, her conversation, or even her name!"

"Indeed," said Ellie again, faintly. With a burst of honesty, she added, "I am afraid you will be disappointed in my taste then, Mr. Garret. For I had been thinking her shawl the loveliest thing in the world!"

"Oh, that's only because you've never had a chance to see real India work," he assured her. "I'll write my uncle and tell him to send over a proper India shawl for you. In fact, I'll have him send you half a dozen."

Ellie looked at him in renewed amazement. He looked back at her, seemingly puzzled by her reaction, but after a moment a flush spread beneath the tan of his cheek. "Only listen to me!" he said. "I'm afraid I'm presuming again, Miss Roswell. I had been taking for granted that I—that we—" He threw Ellie a helpless look.

Ellie could not keep a sparkle out of her eyes, or a smile off her lips. "Much as I might like to, I am afraid I could not accept such a personal gift on such a short acquaintance, Mr. Garret," she said gently. "There are conventions about these things, you know."

"Yes, I do know. I'm not a complete yahoo, though you might be forgiven for thinking it! I know you couldn't accept a personal gift from a man you've only just met." Christopher reached out and took Ellie's hand between his. "But if you have no objection, I would like very much to improve our acquaintance, Miss Roswell. I know it's far too early to speak of such things, but I never met any girl with whom I felt such a—well, such a *connection* as I feel with you. If you would give me permission to call upon you, I would like to see if that connection might not develop into something more."

"I don't see why not," said Ellie, more demurely than ever. "Certainly I would be happy to receive you if you cared to call, Mr. Garret."

For answer, Christopher pressed her hand. Ellie smiled at him, and he smiled back, still holding her hand in his.

"I do care, very much," he said. "So much that I will lose no time availing myself of your kind permission. Expect to see me on your doorstep early tomorrow." He threw Ellie a look half shy and half merry. "And I shall say nothing more on the subject of shawls at present, except to say that I hope someday I may be in a position to give you as many as I like."

Ellie merely smiled in answer to this. She felt the cup of her happiness was filled to overflowing. Later that evening, as she nibbled at rout cakes and drank champagne punch, she could not help reflecting that matters had resolved themselves almost supernally well. The Beales had gotten their goose, she was at the start of a most promising acquaintance with a man who appeared to be her *beau ideal,* and she had been saved from buying a shawl that would have only degraded her in his eyes. "I have been very lucky," she said aloud. "Perhaps there's something in the mince pie after all."

"Mince pie!" said Christopher, catching these last words. "Did you say something about mince pie?"

Coloring, Ellie said she believed she had. Christopher looked from her plate to his. "But we don't have any mince pie," he said. "I would have taken some if there were any. But apparently the Winwoods aren't serving it tonight. They must not believe in the old superstition."

"Superstition?" said Ellie, regarding him with bemusement.

"Yes, the superstition that you'll have good luck in the coming year if you eat mince pie every day during the Christmas Season. My mother used to swear by it. So does Mrs. Merriweather at the Bull, apparently, because she's served it at her table every night so far. But it looks as though tonight my luck is out. Ah, well!" He smiled at Ellie. "I will gladly dispense with mince pie as long as I am lucky enough to be with you."

Ellie was regarding him speculatively. "My mother," she said, "is commonly held to make the best mince pie in the neighborhood."

"Is that so?" said Christopher.

"Yes, it is. And I know for a fact there are at least a dozen pies in our larder at home that haven't been touched as yet."

"Indeed," said Christopher. He, too, was starting to look speculative.

"And we live just a step away from here—right next door, in fact. Mama and Papa and I came by carriage because Mama thinks it more proper than walking for such a formal occasion, but there is no reason why you and I could not walk over just for a minute or two—just as long as it would take to eat a slice of mince pie. Then we could come right back, and you would have assured your good luck for the coming year."

Christopher said this sounded like a fine plan. "It's not that I'm superstitious," he explained. "But I always feel it never hurts to make assurance doubly sure where good fortune is concerned. Besides, I am very fond of mince pie," he added with a smile.

"Then let me talk to Mama and tell her what we propose to do. I am sure she will make no objection, for she is quite a fanatic on the subject of mince pie herself."

Mrs. Roswell, when appealed to, gave a good-humored consent to her daughter's plan. "I've been hearing all about you from Mr. Winwood," she told Christopher. "He says you're just back from India, having been out of the country these ten years or so. It stands to reason you could have gotten no mince pie worthy of the name in India. It would be a shame for you not to have any your first Christmas back. I don't know what the Winwoods are about, not to be serving it tonight," she added in a lower voice. "When I was growing up, my mother made sure it was on the table every night of the Christmas Season, and as long as I've had my own home, I've always made it a point to do the same. If you eat mince pie every day of the Christmas Season, you'll have good luck in the coming year. Everybody knows that."

Christopher said his mother had always said the same thing, which caused Mrs. Roswell to say his mother must have been a sensible woman. "And you're a sensible man, Mr. Garret," she added. "If you and Ellie want to step next door for a few minutes, I don't see there's any harm in it. But are you sure you want to walk? It's a cold night, and it wouldn't be any great trouble to call for the carriage."

Christopher said he did not mind the cold at all. He had no consciousness of speaking an untruth, for with Ellie for a companion, he felt he would have walked miles through the snow and counted it a privilege. And once he had put on his greatcoat and muffler and Ellie her fur-lined boots and woolen cloak, and they were walking along the snowy lane beneath a young moon and a star-spangled sky, the cold was the last thing on his mind.

"What a beautiful night," he said, looking around him. "I don't believe I ever saw a more beautiful night. There's no place like old England, after all."

"I don't suppose there is," said Ellie contentedly. "It *is* a lovely night. So clear, and the moon is so bright it looks like polished silver. I know it's a cliché, but I have always felt there's something magical about a moonlit night."

"And I feel the same," said Christopher. "But there's something rather dangerous about it, too. Surrounded by so much beauty, a man might do any mad thing."

Ellie glanced at him, and found his eyes were resting on her pensively. She hardly knew whether she was glad or sorry when they reached her own front doorstep. There had been a look in Christopher's eye that made her suspect he included her among the beauties of the night, and that he might have kissed her if he had remained longer under their collective influence. She glanced at him shyly, but the moment was clearly past, for he merely reached past her, took up the knocker, and rapped it firmly against the door.

The maid who answered the door seemed surprised to see Ellie there, accompanied by a strange—and very attractive—gentleman. But when Ellie explained her errand, the girl was at once full of solicitude.

"Aye, to be sure you'd be wanting your mince pie, sir! The missus is strong on having mince pie on the table every night, and I know plenty of other folks feel the same. Just you sit down in the parlor with Miss Ellie, sir, and I'll be bringing the two of you a morsel of pie right away."

The parlor, like the rest of the house, was hung with Christmas greenery. Ellie found her eyes dwelling on the sprig of mistletoe suspended over the hearth. She glanced at Christopher to see if he had noticed it, but he was busy looking around the room with an approving smile. "What an attractive room," he said. "It has a homelike look to it. I hope *my* home will look so homelike when once I get settled in it. Oh, and here is our mince pie. I see it's almost midnight, so if we manage matters properly, we can consume our good-luck ration for today *and* tomorrow in one fell swoop."

Ellie made a light reply to this. Together she and Christopher laughed and joked as they ate their mince pie, but all the while she was very much aware that they were alone—as alone as they had been under the sky a few minutes before, now that the maid had gone. And the bunch of mistletoe was still hanging there, right in plain view.

She stole another glance at it, then at Christopher, but he was looking at his plate, now empty except for a few stray crumbs.

"Superb," he declared. "The very best mince pie I have eaten in my life."

"I'm so glad you liked it," said Ellie. "I shall be sure to relay the compliment to Mama." Suddenly nervous, she sprang to her feet. "I suppose we had better be getting back to the Winwoods'."

Christopher agreed, but he took his time putting on his overcoat and muffler. Ellie was ready before he was and stood fidgeting about, trying not to look in the direction of the mistletoe bough. She had just concluded he had failed to notice it when he spoke in an apologetic voice.

"Miss Roswell, you will be thinking me a terribly forward fellow," he said, "but there's a bunch of mistletoe hanging over the hearth there, and I am strongly tempted to take advantage of it. Would you think me an unmitigated bounder if I stole a kiss—just one kiss, for luck?"

"No," said Ellie in a soft voice. "I would not think you a bounder at all."

Putting an arm about her shoulders, Christopher led her beneath the bough, bent down, and touched his lips to hers. "That should do it," he said with satisfaction. "Mince pie and mistletoe! Now I have my full complement of luck for the coming year."

Ellie laughed. She felt life and love and happiness pulsing through her veins. "It was my pleasure," she said, dimpling up at him. "Merry Christmas, Mr. Garret."

"Merry Christmas, Miss Roswell," he replied. And then proceeding, no doubt, on the assumption that no one can have too much good luck, he bent down and kissed her again.

A Note on Mince Pies

Mince pie fillings vary widely and are not necessarily synonymous with the mincemeat we nowadays tend to associate with the holidays. The recipe below contains no meat in any form. It did originally contain suet, but I find butter works well as a substitute and will probably be more to the taste of modern American readers. Suet can, however, be used if you prefer and if you know a reliable source for it. In my area it is sold mainly for the purpose of feeding wild birds and is packaged and processed accordingly.

Let me note here, also, that I have no proof that good luck will result from the consumption of this pie during the holiday season. But since consuming it is such a pleasant and painless process, you may consider that you have nothing to lose by trying!

LEMON MINCE PIE

1 lb. short-crust pastry (enough for a 2-crust 9" pie)

Filling:

Approximately 6 cups of peeled and chopped cooking apples such as Red Rome, Golden Delicious, or Granny Smith
1 c. raisins
¾ c. sugar
¼ c. lemon juice
2 T. grated lemon peel
2 T. tapioca (this, too, is a deviation from the original recipe, but I think it improves it, especially if the apples are very juicy)
1 tsp. nutmeg
½ tsp. mace
¼ pound (1 stick) butter

Extra sugar for sprinkling top crust

Preheat oven to 400 degress F (375 degrees F if you are using a glass pie plate). Melt butter and combine with other filling ingredients. Pour into prepared unbaked short crust. Top with other crust, crimp edges, and slash top to allow steam to escape as mixture bakes (for a pretty touch, use decorative cookie cutters to cut stars, bells, or other holiday motifs in top crust). Sprinkle top of pie with sugar. Bake 40 to 55 minutes, until apples are tender and crust is golden brown. Serve warm or cold.

More Zebra Regency Romances